Why Women Win at Bridge

Danny Roth is the author of *Clues to Winning Play: Detective Work in Bridge* (1987), *Signal Success in Bridge* (1989), *Awareness: The Way to Improve Your Bridge* (1991) and *Bridge: Groundwork in Play and Defence* (1992).

Why Women Win at Bridge

DANNY ROTH

faber and faber
LONDON · BOSTON

First published in 1992
by Faber and Faber Limited
3 Queen Square London WCIN 3AU

Photoset by Parker Typesetting Service, Leicester
Printed in England by Clays Ltd, St Ives plc

A CIP record for this book is available from the British Library

ISBN 0-571-16748-9

Contents

	Foreword by Michelle R. Brunner	vii
	Introduction	ix
1	Modesty	1
2	Truth Economics	6
3	God Save the Queen	14
4	Very Particular	21
5	Perusing the Tabloids	30
6	Uncharted Waters	36
7	Panorama	42
8	Harmony and Balance	46
9	The Crystal Ball	54
10	Accepting Limitations	57
11	That Good Old Intuition	61
12	Time for Oneself	64
13	Fitting in	68
14	Charity Begins at Home	74
15	Feeling the Pinch	84
16	Cornering	91
17	Battle on the Plain	96
18	Rose-coloured Spectacles	104
	Conclusion	114

Foreword

When Danny first told me of his intention to write a book entitled *Why Women Win at Bridge*, I envisaged it being the shortest book ever written. One would open the cover and find a solitary page ... 'Because all females who play duplicate against Danny Roth always get two tops!'

Of course, as suggested by the title, this book is in fact a direct reply to *Why Women Lose at Bridge* by the Australian bridge player, Joyce Nicholson, which was published in the Master Bridge Series in 1985. The book insinuated, among other things, that women are incapable of performing well at the bridge table as they have too much else to think about.

It is quite ironic that, while a woman should denounce her own sex's capabilities in this field, a man should defend them, and Danny has gone to great lengths to do just that. The book is illustrated by a collection of genuine bridge hands, all played or defended by women, whose identities are to remain a closely guarded secret.

Danny has already written several successful books on bridge and enjoys modest success at the bridge table too (provided, of course, that he does not play against any women).

Michelle R. Brunner
February 1992

Introduction

Joyce Nicholson's *Why Woman Lose at Bridge* (1985) suggested that women had relatively little chance of performing as well at bridge as men because of their comparatively disadvantaged place in society. To reach her conclusion, Nicholson had contacted large numbers of bridge players of both sexes and amassed data about various relevant factors, notably amounts of time and energy devoted to the game. To summarize, the book pointed to:

1 Women's lack of aggression, lack of competitiveness, lack of determination to win, lack of concentration and lack of stamina. It was even held by some that the necessary killer instinct was not 'ladylike', men preferring their prospective wives to be a little inferior.

2 Women's heavy commitment to family responsibilities and therefore their lack of the single-mindedness necessary to reach the top.

3 The fact that women do not play enough bridge in the early years of their lives, when their education is preparing them to be good wives and mothers.

4 The fact that women's dependence on men – notably in the financial field – means a lack of freedom and less need to take decisions (although 74 per cent of the women who replied described their husbands as very supportive and 11 per cent were single at the time of answering; 82 per cent claimed to have no money problems).

5   The fact that women are more tolerant of error and defeat, and less compelled to strive for perfection in what, even at world level, is only a game.

Seven years on, such ideas seem strangely dated, but even at the time, the arguments were flawed. Nicholson used as ammunition the fact that a lot of women tend to play 'social' bridge, when the social aspect is what tends to be emphasized and their thoughts might well be focused as much on the latest gossip, what the children are doing upstairs or what is in the oven as on who holds the six of diamonds. But if we are talking stereotypes, what about the men who play bridge at their clubs as a form of relaxation after a 'hard day at the office', often following a splendid alcohol-enhanced dinner? It is equally unlikely that they are in the best frame of mind to concentrate wholeheartedly.

Men or women, these people are not serious bridge players. They enjoy the game precisely for its social aspects; they do not care enormously about winning and nor do they have great aspirations to become better players. Indeed, if they were to become better players, they might well lose some of the social benefits they currently enjoy.

This book, however, is concerned with aspiring and top-level players. There are a number of female bridge professionals well respected throughout the world – the late Rixi Markus and Dorothy Truscott are perhaps the best known. Indeed, most of the top female players in America are professionals, earning their living by playing with clients, both as partners and team-mates. And the top female partnerships spend just as much time as their male counterparts perfecting their bidding and their defensive signalling systems.

Times are changing. In the past, many of the reasons Joyce Nicholson found for the failure of women to reach the top might well have applied. In bridge, as in other endeavours, women were not encouraged to succeed, and no doubt spent more time concerned with family matters. However, the trend has been changing for some time. Women now have more choice about how to lead their lives, and, as a result, they have greater expectations. Just as today we can see increasing numbers of women succeeding in areas such as industry, business and politics, so in the formerly male preserve of bridge, more women are coming to the fore.

In 1984 the British Grand Masters pairs was won by two women, Sandra Landy and Sally Horton, and in the same year the winning team in the Gold Cup, Britain's toughest knock-out teams competition, included three women. The winning teams in 1989, 1990 and 1991 included at least one woman. It is true that an all-female team has yet to be successful – indeed, it is doubtful whether an all-female team has even entered the competition. However, the fact that, in recent years, women have been members of winning teams points towards the recognition by the top male players that there are women who are good enough to join their ranks.

And it is not only in the playing of the game that women are becoming successful. In his foreword to *Why Women Lose at Bridge*, Hugh Kelsey wrote:

> The question of why men are usually selected as non-playing captains of women's teams is a puzzling one, and it is interesting to speculate on reactions if a woman were to be appointed as captain of a men's team. To the best of my knowledge this has never happened, nor it is likely to happen.

In 1991 the captain of the women's team, USA II, which won the world championship, was Kathie Wei. Even more remarkably, also in that year, Great Britain chose Sandra Landy to be the captain of their open team for the European championship and Great Britain won that event in convincing style. It was their first victory since 1963.

In 1989 a marathon duplicate bridge match was staged between men and women, placing one table in New York and the other in Paris. It was a charity event and money was raised by selling tickets which entitled the purchaser to play for one hour. Although some top-class players did participate, the vast majority, male and female, were ordinary club players. It was an extremely close affair. Play continued round the clock for a solid fortnight, during which 2,352 boards were completed. At the end, the men won by 200 International Match Points (IMPs), the equivalent of less than 0.1 IMPs per deal. The number of deals played in a world championship final has varied over the years, but has only twice been won by a margin of less than 0.1 IMPs per deal. During the match, the lead changed hands a number of times, and had the match been of between 1,300 and 1,500 deals, the women would have won.

This book demonstrates that, once and for all in every area of the game, there are now countless examples of women playing bridge just as well as their male counterparts.

Modesty

One factor that works strongly against the male bridge player is machismo. Perhaps the traditional courtship ritual of making himself attractive while he begins his approach, trying to impress the woman with some sort of 'show', lies behind the man's compulsive urge 'to play to the gallery'. While the woman is often happy to keep it simple, for the man the more spectacular the better.

This tendency is particularly noticeable in the areas of deceptive cardplay and psychic bidding. There are many male examples of defensive cardplay which are designed to fool declarer but actually succeed only in fooling partner. The first concern to a woman is usually to help her partner, and only when she is sure that her partner cannot be confused will she then focus her mind on deceiving declarer.

The worst that a confused defender can do is to allow a contract which could have been defeated to be made. There is, however, scope for much greater disaster in the area of psychic bidding. Several decades ago, a hand was reported in which a notorious psychic-bid fanatic, playing rubber bridge, sitting South, dealt himself a full suit of hearts at Game All. Terrified of a cheap sacrifice in spades against his cold grand slam (and there was no guarantee that seven spades was going off at all), he psyched in spades! His partner, with a modest spade fit and a solid minor, promptly propelled him into the wrong grand slam and confidently redoubled the inevitable double. As it turned out, declarer did not take a single trick and, with the doubler producing the four top spades, conceded a record 7,700 penalty.

The post-mortem (during which South mentioned the famous Vanderbilt hand when a thirteen-of-a-suit grand slam in spades was overcalled with seven no-trumps – a contract which could not be defeated because the other hand was on lead) does not bear repeating, but one cannot help feeling that, had a woman occupied that South seat, she would have opened a simple seven hearts, prepared to collect any penalty available if she was outbid. That is, of course, not to mention removing seven spades redoubled to seven no-trumps to save a few thousand points as the auction actually proceeded!

That does not, of course, mean that women are debarred from the world of psychology. It is accepted that the American player Dorothy Sims (1889–1960) is the 'mother' of the psychic bid and, perhaps embarrassed that they didn't think of it first, men have tried to make up for it by carrying the idea too far.

While we are on the subject of very distributional hands, take a look at this. Sitting East in a teams-of-four match, you hold:

♠ —   ♥ A K Q 7 5 3   ♦ 10 9 7 6 2   ♣ A 4

Your partner deals, non-vulnerable against vulnerable opponents, and opens a natural one club. North overcalls with one spade and you decide to make a negative double. On this occasion, the woman sitting South is kind enough to warn you that she has the hearts heavily stacked against you when she bids two hearts. This is passed round to you. What action do you take?

At this vulnerability, it seems sensible to take a penalty when a game would be worth only about 400 anyway. So you let it stand and, following a far-from-perfect defence, you emerge with eleven tricks to score +600, the full deal and auction being:

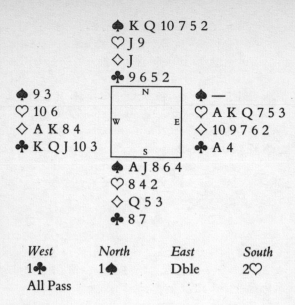

♠ K Q 10 7 5 2
♡ J 9
♢ J
♣ 9 6 5 2

♠ 9 3
♡ 10 6
♢ A K 8 4
♣ K Q J 10 3

♠ —
♡ A K Q 7 5 3
♢ 10 9 7 6 2
♣ A 4

♠ A J 8 6 4
♡ 8 4 2
♢ Q 5 3
♣ 8 7

West	North	East	South
1♣	1♠	Dble	2♡
All Pass			

The defence usually goes wrong in very heavy defeats and you
have been talked out of a grand slam in clubs or hearts with
seven diamonds depending on the correct play in trumps. But
observe the contrast. The woman psychs in hearts, prepared to
go back to spades if necessary, while the man psychs in spades,
from which, at the grand slam level, there is no sensible escape.

Reports abound of male players losing fortunes through
trying to be clever. Similar cases involving women are very rare.

However, 'playing to the gallery' need not have catastrophic
consequences, provided players ensure 'safety first'. In a teams-
of-four match, North dealt with East–West vulnerable:

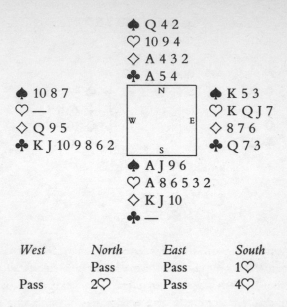

♠ Q 4 2
♡ 10 9 4
◇ A 4 3 2
♣ A 5 4

♠ 10 8 7
♡ —
◇ Q 9 5
♣ K J 10 9 8 6 2

♠ K 5 3
♡ K Q J 7
◇ 8 7 6
♣ Q 7 3

♠ A J 9 6
♡ A 8 6 5 3 2
◇ K J 10
♣ —

West	North	East	South
	Pass	Pass	1♡
Pass	2♡	Pass	4♡

After two passes, South opened one heart and West passed, discouraged by the adverse vulnerability. North raised to two hearts, which showed 6–10 points and exactly three hearts (the pair were playing a response of one no-trump as forcing and could describe other hands via that bid). East passed again and South bought the contract in four hearts.

West did well to find the best lead of the ten of clubs (promising two higher honours). Short of entries to the table, the woman sitting South won immediately in dummy, discarding the ten of diamonds from hand. Spades would have to be attacked sooner or later, so she led the two of spades to the jack and followed with the ace and a low card to the queen and king. East returned the queen of clubs, which South ruffed. She now made the key play of a low heart towards the ten. West discarded a club while East won and returned another club, ruffed by South to leave this position:

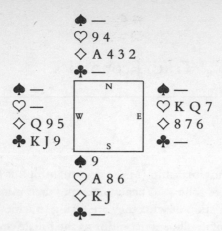

```
              ♠ —
              ♡ 9 4
              ◇ A 4 3 2
              ♣ —
  ♠ —          ┌─────────┐      ♠ —
  ♡ —          │    N    │      ♡ K Q 7
  ◇ Q 9 5    W │         │ E    ◇ 8 7 6
  ♣ K J 9      │    S    │      ♣ —
              └─────────┘
              ♠ 9
              ♡ A 8 6
              ◇ K J
              ♣ —
```

At this point, it would have been good enough to cross to the ace of diamonds and lead the four of hearts to ensure the loss of one further heart trick only, or play a low heart to the nine and East's queen, subsequently picking up East's remaining trumps with a simple finesse, However, should East have had a club left in this position, admittedly unlikely on the play of the suit so far, these lines would have been unsuccessful because East would play a club when in with his trump. Declarer would have to ruff and would then be unable to draw East's last trump. Our heroine found a better line, which was also designed to entertain the crowd. She cashed the king and ace of diamonds and ruffed a third round in hand. Now she ruffed the nine of spades with the nine of hearts and East, forced to overruff, had to lead from her ♡K-7 into declarer's ♡A-8.

This hand was a good illustration of anticipating trouble well in advance but was all very hard work for a flat board! At the other table, defending the same contract, her team-mate in the West seat led a low diamond, giving declarer (a man) a free finesse in the suit. South laid down the ace of hearts to give the enemy three trump tricks, but the even diamond split allowed declarer to discard two losing spades on the ace of clubs and fourth diamond.

Truth Economics

This kind of showmanship (or showwomanship!) is but a fore-taste of what is to follow. When women put their mind to it, and have a clear intention of what they are trying to achieve, they are just as capable of intelligent deception as their male counterparts.

Watch a female defender (partnering her husband) resort to deception to defeat a declarer who has landed in the wrong contract following a bidding misunderstanding – yes, in a world championship match. It happens all too often! West dealt, non-vulnerable against vulnerable opponents, at teams-of-four.

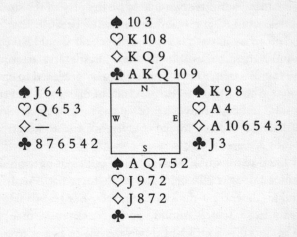

♠ 10 3
♡ K 10 8
◇ K Q 9
♣ A K Q 10 9

♠ J 6 4   ♠ K 9 8
♡ Q 6 5 3   ♡ A 4
◇ —   ◇ A 10 6 5 4 3
♣ 8 7 6 5 4 2   ♣ J 3

♠ A Q 7 5 2
♡ J 9 7 2
◇ J 8 7 2
♣ —

West	North	East	South
Pass	1♣	1♢	1♠
Pass	2NT	Pass	3♡
Pass	4♡	All Pass	

The dealer passed and North opened one club. East overcalled with one diamond and South bid one spade. West passed (probably with some relief!) and North responded two no-trumps. East passed and South now made the mistake of bidding three hearts. South's length in diamonds, combined with North's strength in the suit, virtually guaranteed a singleton or void with West and the danger of ruffs in a major-suit game, even if an eight-card fit existed. If North had had any interest in playing in hearts, she could have bid the suit herself, or possibly cue-bid two diamonds. Hence, as the auction went, she naturally credited her partner with a five-card heart suit and raised to game.

West led the five of clubs, confirming his diamond void, and, satisfied that West had most of the outstanding clubs, South finessed the nine. East produced the jack and South had to ruff. Now a low heart ran to the eight and ace and East cashed her ace of diamonds. A diamond ruff seemed the obvious move at this point but the woman sitting East first considered the consequences. It was clear that the defence would now take a second trump trick but equally clear that this would be all. Instead, therefore, she switched to the nine of spades. To South, this was an obvious singleton, so he rose with the ace and prayed for an even trump split, only to find that he could not avoid losing to the queen of hearts and king of spades to go one off.

In this next example, a woman gave the impression of wealth when all she had was an empty jewel case.

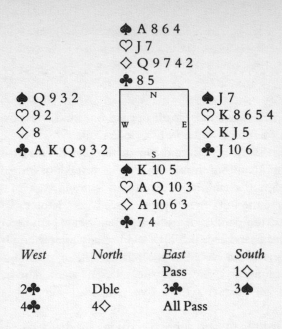

♠ A 8 6 4
♡ J 7
◇ Q 9 7 4 2
♣ 8 5

♠ Q 9 3 2
♡ 9 2
◇ 8
♣ A K Q 9 3 2

♠ J 7
♡ K 8 6 5 4
◇ K J 5
♣ J 10 6

♠ K 10 5
♡ A Q 10 3
◇ A 10 6 3
♣ 7 4

West	North	East	South
		Pass	1◇
2♣	Dble	3♣	3♠
4♣	4◇	All Pass	

East dealt at Love All in a world mixed-pairs event, with the men, a world-famous partnership in open events, sitting East and South.

The dealer passed and South, playing five-card majors, opened one diamond. West overcalled with two clubs and North made a negative double. East pushed up to three clubs and South bid three hearts. West persisted with four clubs but North bid four diamonds to buy the contract.

West led the ace of clubs, East following with the jack. West now played a low club to her partner's ten and East switched to a low heart. This ran round to the jack and South took a second successful heart finesse. Now came the ace of hearts and the spotlight shifted to West. Sensibly deciding that a discard would be of little value to declarer, West meanly clung on to her trump, discarding a club to avoid giving information about the trump position. South naturally decided that West was hanging on to a 'useful' trump holding and cashed the ace of diamonds, followed by another trump, only to find himself two light and with a well below average score – most annoying when +300 was available in four clubs doubled!

The ability of a defender to give the wrong impression of a holding in a particular suit has been the undoing of many a declarer. Here is an example of a jumping jack.

One of America's leading ladies picked up the following hand in a teams' championship:

♠ J 6 2   ♡ J 6   ◇ Q 8 2   ♣ A 10 8 7 3

It was therefore a little surprising that, after North had dealt at Game All, the opponents galloped into the slam zone.

This was the full deal:

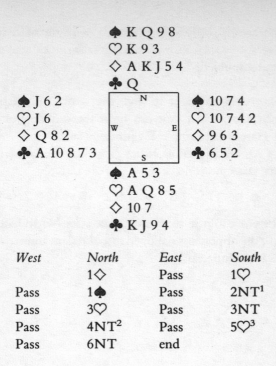

♠ K Q 9 8
♡ K 9 3
♢ A K J 5 4
♣ Q

♠ J 6 2
♡ J 6
♢ Q 8 2
♣ A 10 8 7 3

♠ 10 7 4
♡ 10 7 4 2
♢ 9 6 3
♣ 6 5 2

♠ A 5 3
♡ A Q 8 5
♢ 10 7
♣ K J 9 4

West	North	East	South
	1♢	Pass	1♡
Pass	1♠	Pass	2NT[1]
Pass	3♡	Pass	3NT
Pass	4NT[2]	Pass	5♡[3]
Pass	6NT	end	

[1] This bid was forcing in their system.
[2] Quantitative in principle but could be taken as Blackwood if partner considered it appropriate.
[3] Showing two aces.

West pondered some time over her opening lead. Thinking that, if her partner held ♠10-x-x-x and declarer a doubleton honour, there might be scope for deception, she tossed the jack of spades on the table.

There were various chances in all four suits. In both majors, declarer could have tried for the break or a restricted-choice finesse. There was also the diamond finesse and the chance of the ten of clubs dropping in three rounds, not to mention a number of squeeze possibilities. Declarer won in dummy and played the queen of clubs, which was allowed to hold. Now South led the nine of hearts (an unblock, necessary if he decided to take a finesse against East later), winning with the queen in hand. Then came the king of clubs, which West won and switched to the two of diamonds. South won with dummy's king, led a spade to the ace and cashed the jack of clubs. With the ten failing to appear, declarer was faced with a decision in this position:

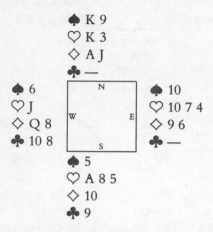

The red-suit position was as yet unclear but, when South led his last spade and West followed, it was 'obvious' that the lead had come from ♠ J-10-x-x and that the finesse was right. South therefore called for the nine, failing in a contract he could have made in several ways. In fact, if he guesses all three non-club suits correctly, he can make an overtrick!

Bertrand Russell is often quoted as saying: 'Obviousness is always the enemy of correctness.' The next example was more than obvious to declarer but turned out to be another empty threat. Here was a bomb which did no more than dissipate heavy smoke – but with destructive effect.

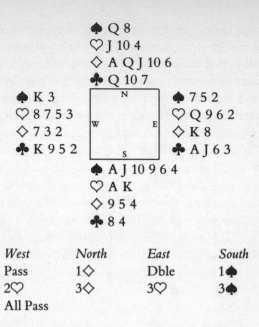

♠ Q 8
♡ J 10 4
♢ A Q J 10 6
♣ Q 10 7

♠ K 3
♡ 8 7 5 3
♢ 7 3 2
♣ K 9 5 2

♠ 7 5 2
♡ Q 9 6 2
♢ K 8
♣ A J 6 3

♠ A J 10 9 6 4
♡ A K
♢ 9 5 4
♣ 8 4

West	North	East	South
Pass	1♢	Dble	1♠
2♡	3♢	3♡	3♠
All Pass			

In a pairs event, West dealt at Love All and passed. North (actually playing a strong one-club style) opened one diamond, which may have been a short suit, but not on this occasion. East doubled, showing at least two four-card suits outside diamonds. With only ten points, including a king in the opponent's suit, this action is questionable, but many players feel it is worth competing light at this type of scoring. South bid one spade, forcing. West came in with two hearts. North competed with three diamonds – again questionable. Having already more than shown her hand, East decided to bid it again, supporting to three hearts and now South made the even more surprising bid of three spades. Surely he was obliged to insist on game. Perhaps he thought three spades was forcing. Anyway, that was the final contract and, however outrageous the bidding was, it was a mere hors-d'oeuvre compared with the play! Just watch this.

West led the two of clubs to her partner's jack. Beginners are told that one of the most basic offences is to blank a king but with respect for the monarchy rapidly disappearing nowadays, East lost no time in returning the eight of diamonds! To declarer, this was an 'obvious' singleton and, on that assumption, he thought that his contract was safe as long as he did not concede two diamond ruffs. Accordingly, he spurned the trump finesse (usually advisable in this type of situation) and played out ace and another. West won and sent back a diamond. North finessed against the 'marked' king only to find him offside, whereupon East returned a low club to her partner's king and received her diamond ruff for one off. That was hard work for a board only just above average with many of the rest of the field losing the obvious four tricks in four spades – a 75 per cent contract which fails because the two finesses are both wrong.

This was a brilliant defence by any standards and South could have saved himself only by putting a question mark against that opening lead. He could see twenty-four points, leaving sixteen for the defenders. Once West had shown the king of spades and had been credited with the king of diamonds, the remaining points had to be with East if the double made any sense at all. That would mean that East would have to hold all three club honours, implying that the two of clubs would have come from three or four small cards – an unlikely lead after hearts had been supported. Admittedly, this is very subtle analysis but against defence of that calibre, you have to be that meticulous.

God Save the Queen

All good card players, whatever their sex, pride themselves on their ability to locate missing queens. Any such guess has a considerably greater than 50 per cent chance of success. Consequently, the defenders' role is often one of protecting their queen – either by shrouding its whereabouts or defending in such a way that they cannot be prevented from scoring it.

The first example illustrates a deal in which the bidding succeeded in misleading declarer as to the whereabouts of a crucial missing queen.

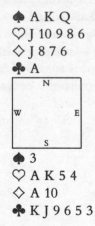

♠ A K Q
♡ J 10 9 8 6
♢ J 8 7 6
♣ A

♠ 3
♡ A K 5 4
♢ A 10
♣ K J 9 6 5 3

West	North	East	South
			1♣
3♠	Dble	Pass	4♡
Pass	4♠	Pass	4NT
Pass	5♡	Pass	5NT
Pass	6♢	Pass	7♡
All Pass			

In a women's teams-of-four match, South dealt, vulnerable against not. The dealer opened one club and West came in with three spades, a pre-emptive bid on a suit which, as North could see, was of inferior quality but which was likely to throw the opposition off the rails. North doubled, primarily for take-out and, when East passed, South bid four hearts. West passed and North cue-bid four spades. East passed and South bid a Blackwood four no-trumps. North's five hearts showed two aces and South's five no-trumps asked for kings. North's six diamonds showed one king and South bid seven hearts.

West's diamond lead ran to the queen and ace. Any ideas on the play? Declarer realized that if hearts were not breaking, as was probable on the bidding, an extra club trick would have to be set up to look after the last losing diamond. Accordingly, she crossed to the ace of clubs, cashed two high spades, discarding a diamond, played a heart to the ace and ruffed a low club, intending to follow with the trump finesse. She would then draw the last trump, ruff another club and claim. However, this was the full deal:

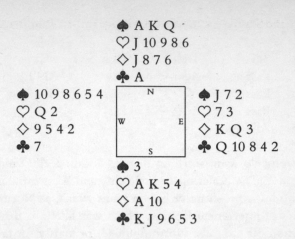

♠ A K Q
♡ J 10 9 8 6
♦ J 8 7 6
♣ A

♠ 10 9 8 6 5 4   ♠ J 7 2
♡ Q 2   ♡ 7 3
♦ 9 5 4 2   ♦ K Q 3
♣ 7   ♣ Q 10 8 4 2

♠ 3
♡ A K 5 4
♦ A 10
♣ K J 9 6 5 3

When declarer tried to take her first club ruff, West ruffed in with the queen of hearts and declarer had to go one down. Had West not bid, no doubt declarer would have followed the normal 'eight-never, nine-never' rule and cashed the ace and king of hearts, after which the contract can be claimed.

One of the world's leading male players, Zia Mahmood, recommends making take-out doubles when holding Q-x in opener's suit; declarer will usually credit you with a singleton and misguess the trumps in similar situations. As you see, women can also indulge in such deceptions. Notice that East refrained from supporting the spades. She did not want to suggest a sacrifice (which would probably not have been profitable on the new scoring scale anyway) as she had some defensive prospects.

Take the South seat at Game All in a teams-of-four match.

♠ K Q 10 8 5
♡ Q 8 5 3
◇ K J 6
♣ 6

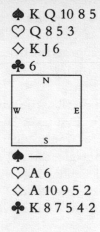

♠ —
♡ A 6
◇ A 10 9 5 2
♣ K 8 7 5 4 2

West	North	East	South
	1♠	Pass	2◇
Pass	2♡	Pass	3♣
Pass	3◇	Pass	5◇
All Pass			

Your partner deals and opens one spade, playing five-card majors. The opposition are silent and, playing canapé-style responses, you reply with two diamonds. After two hearts from partner, you bid three clubs. In this system, the bid is natural, rather than 'fourth-suit', but still forcing. Partner gives preference to three diamonds and you, rather optimistically, jump to five diamonds. How do you play on the lead of the four of diamonds?

Hasty play to the first trick is often the cause of many unnecessary defeats and it will be wise to work out the whole hand before calling for a card from dummy. It is clear that you will need to set up the clubs and that they are probably going to have to be 3–3 with the ace well placed in the East hand. In any case, the first lead will have to come from dummy and thus, if you accept the free finesse in trumps, you will have to win the first trick in hand and play a second trump in order to return to dummy. Now, if the ace of clubs is in the same hand as the outstanding trump, the appropriate defender will be able to play a killing third round of trumps, leaving you to lose at least two club tricks and a heart.

To avoid this, you play well to rise with the king of diamonds and attack clubs at once. East takes her ace and returns a low heart. It costs nothing for you to duck, so you play low and West takes her king, returning the suit to your ace. You ruff a club in dummy, both defenders following, and run the jack of diamonds, hoping that the breaks are 3–2 in trumps and 3–3 in clubs and so indeed they are – but down you go – the full deal being:

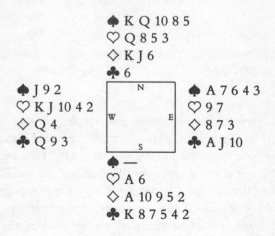

The opening lead had left the queen bare. At first sight, it looks as though West had done all she could to *help* declarer locate the queen of trumps. In practice, however, on most leads, declarer needs to ruff two clubs in dummy and would have no option but to play down the ace and king of trumps which would have dropped West's queen. Alternatively, if East switches to a trump when on lead with the ace of clubs, the trump position is even more revealing.

It is fitting that, in a recent Bols Tip competition, one of the best contributions came from a woman – actually one of Britain's former world champions: words to the effect of 'If the bidding calls for a trump lead, do not be afraid to lead one, even if it has to be from an uninviting holding.'

Here an unsuspecting declarer was treated to a phantom crash in a coup which won a major award; it is noteworthy that not only was a woman responsible for a cruel false-card but a female world champion was on the receiving end! The two players concerned were sitting West and South, partnered by their respective husbands in a world-wide pairs contest.

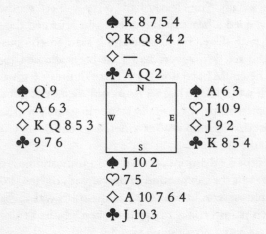

♠ K 8 7 5 4
♡ K Q 8 4 2
♢ —
♣ A Q 2

♠ Q 9
♡ A 6 3
♢ K Q 8 5 3
♣ 9 7 6

♠ A 6 3
♡ J 10 9
♢ J 9 2
♣ K 8 5 4

♠ J 10 2
♡ 7 5
♢ A 10 7 6 4
♣ J 10 3

West	North	East	South
		Pass	Pass
1♢	Dble	1NT	Pass
2♢	3♢	Pass	3NT
Pass	4♢	Pass	4♣
All Pass			

East dealt at Love All and, after two passes, West opened one diamond and North doubled. East bid one no-trump, South passed and West rebid two diamonds, leaving North with something of a problem. He was clearly worth another bid, but to bid either major would overstate the suit quality and understate his suitability for playing elsewhere. Alternatively, to make a second take-out double could also lead to disaster with such a shapely hand. Consequently, he decided to overbid with a cue-bid of three diamonds. Not quite sure what to make of this, South showed her diamond guard but, when North rebid four diamonds, it became obvious that he had a major two-suiter, so she corrected to four spades. This was an interesting sequence, but nowhere near as fascinating as the play.

West led the king of diamonds, South winning as dummy discarded a club. She clearly had to try and set up the dummy hand so she led a heart to the queen and returned the suit. East followed with the jack and nine and it seemed obvious for West to play the six. However, had East been allowed to hold the trick, all he could have done was force dummy with a diamond and South would have been able to ruff the hearts good and lead the jack of trumps, eventually conceding only a trump and a club. For that reason, West offered a Greek gift, smoothly tossing in the ace.

She returned a diamond, ruffed in dummy and now South felt obliged to ruff the next round of hearts with the ten, hoping that the club finesse would work. Now the truth was revealed, after which two trump tricks, as well as the club, had to be lost and the contract could no longer be made.

4

Very Particular

A well-known film-star once said of the legendary director Alfred Hitchock that, if he was directing a crowd scene involving 30,000 people and one actor had one shirt-button undone, he would spot it! Hitchcock was, however, very much the exception. It is normally the female who is meticulous. This can be very important at the bridge table, and how often has the importance of the significance of small cards been emphasized?

Much has been written, particularly in literature on defence, about the functions of lower cards and one of the most important is to protect their seniors from capture. It is therefore infuriating to find that opposing women can turn this very fact to their advantage.

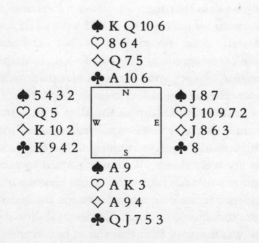

```
              ♠ K Q 10 6
              ♡ 8 6 4
              ◇ Q 7 5
              ♣ A 10 6
♠ 5 4 3 2        N        ♠ J 8 7
♡ Q 5                     ♡ J 10 9 7 2
◇ K 10 2    W        E    ◇ J 8 6 3
♣ K 9 4 2        S        ♣ 8
              ♠ A 9
              ♡ A K 3
              ◇ A 9 4
              ♣ Q J 7 5 3
```

West	North	East	South
			1♣
Pass	1NT	Pass	2NT
Pass	3♣	Pass	3◇
Pass	3♠	Pass	4♣
Pass	5♣	Pass	6♣
All Pass			

In a women's world teams final, South dealt, with East–West vulnerable. With East–West silent throughout, South opened a strong one club and North replied with one no-trump, showing 8–13 points, balanced and forcing to game. South showed that she too had a balanced hand with two no-trumps and North investigated further with a five-card Stayman three clubs. When South responded three diamonds, she showed her major with three spades. So far, South had promised only sixteen points, and with eighteen, a five-card suit and such good controls, she felt obliged to do more than simply sign off in three no-trumps. Accordingly, she tried an ambiguous four clubs, either natural, showing a five-card suit, or a cue-bid in support of spades. North had extra values and was happy to cooperate in looking for a black-suit slam. She therefore made the encouraging bid of five clubs – with no interest she would have rebid four spades. South had really done enough by now, but she knew that her partner didn't have anything else to cue-bid, so decided to bid the slam anyway. Never mind – it is the play that matters!

West was already in difficulties at trick one. With the opponents having crawled up to the slam with a trump stack against them, passive defence was clearly called for and she started with a spade, the five running to the ten, jack and ace. When dummy went down, West was pleased to note that the king of trumps could not be caught. South played a trump to the ten and returned to the nine of spades to run the queen of clubs. East's failure to follow confirmed the inescapability of the trump loser, but it was this very loser that was to be turned to declarer's advantage. She cashed the ace and king of hearts, crossed to the ace of trumps and cashed the two remaining spades, discarding a heart and a diamond from hand. She now ruffed a heart. West was caught – he could either overruff now and be forced to lead a diamond, or discard a diamond and wait until the next trick to be thrown in.

In this next example, the relative weights of the smaller cards decided the fate of a redoubled contract.

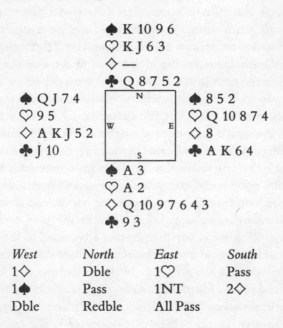

	♠ K 10 9 6		
	♡ K J 6 3		
	◇ —		
	♣ Q 8 7 5 2		
♠ Q J 7 4		♠ 8 5 2
♡ 9 5		♡ Q 10 8 7 4
◇ A K J 5 2		◇ 8
♣ J 10		♣ A K 6 4
	♠ A 3		
	♡ A 2		
	◇ Q 10 9 7 6 4 3		
	♣ 9 3		

West	North	East	South
1◇	Dble	1♡	Pass
1♠	Pass	1NT	2◇
Dble	Redble	All Pass	

In a women's pairs contest, West dealt at Love All and opened one diamond, which North doubled. East bid one heart and South had a problem. Although she had more than sufficient values to warrant a bid, a bid of two diamonds would have had a conventional meaning, so she chose to pass for the moment. West rebid one spade and when North passed, East bid one no-trump. This clearly indicated that both pairs had misfits, but nevertheless South felt that her reasonable seven-card suit and two aces warranted some action, so she came in with two diamonds. West gratefully doubled and North redoubled for rescue. South felt that she had nowhere to go and stood it, prepared for an outright top or bottom.

West led nine of hearts to the jack, queen and ace. South started on trumps with the nine which was allowed to hold and the six was won by the jack, West continuing hearts to dummy's king. South re-entered her hand with the ace of spades and led the queen of diamonds to West's king. West now switched to the jack of clubs and when dummy played low, the woman sitting East played well to overtake with the king and push through the ten of hearts. South discarded her club loser and West also discarded a club. On the next heart, South ruffed with the seven and West refused to overruff. South was now able to cross to the king of spades and ruff a spade but West sat over her ◇10–4 at the finish with ◇A–5 and the contract was defeated for 200 to East–West.

South could have vindicated her bidding by trying to make her trumps by ruffing rather than drawing the opponents'. Indeed, it is usually good technique (and this applies to both sides) that, if there are long trumps in two opposing hands, one should try to take as many ruffs as possible early in the play to avoid an endplay. With the spade distribution advertised in the bidding, she should have won the first heart in hand and cashed the two top spades, ruffing a third round. Now she crosses to the king of hearts and plays a fourth round of spades. East can do her best by ruffing in with the eight but South overruffs and, having taken six tricks already, is still holding ◇Q–10–7–6–4. She exits in clubs and cannot be prevented from taking two more tricks in trumps to take her total to eight.

A woman's meticulous attention to detail struck again on this next example. When defending against her, one has to be careful to avoid even the tiniest patches of ice, otherwise she is likely to benefit from a minor slip.

In a world pairs contest, North dealt with East–West vulnerable.

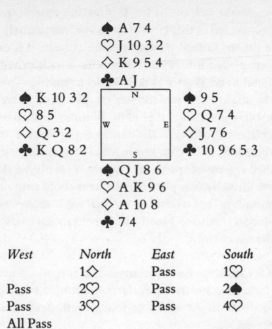

```
              ♠ A 7 4
              ♡ J 10 3 2
              ◇ K 9 5 4
              ♣ A J
  ♠ K 10 3 2    N      ♠ 9 5
  ♡ 8 5                ♡ Q 7 4
  ◇ Q 3 2   W     E    ◇ J 7 6
  ♣ K Q 8 2            ♣ 10 9 6 5 3
                S
              ♠ Q J 8 6
              ♡ A K 9 6
              ◇ A 10 8
              ♣ 7 4
```

West	North	East	South
	1◇	Pass	1♡
Pass	2♡	Pass	2♠
Pass	3♡	Pass	4♡
All Pass			

At several tables, where the dealer opened with a weak no-trump, North played in four hearts after a Stayman sequence. Where East led a spade, North could easily set up an extra trick in that suit, or in diamonds, for a club discard and eleven tricks. At this table, however, North–South were playing a strong no-trump with five-card majors and, as a result, North had to open one diamond. Thus South was the first to mention the heart suit and she now became declarer in the game contract.

West produced the more testing lead of the king of clubs and the defenders were a move ahead. Our declarer had to give them a chance to back-pedal. She won the first trick and, with a shortage of entries in dummy, decided to abandon the possibility of West holding a singleton queen and finessed in trumps immediately, drawing them in three rounds, West discarding a club on the third.

Now came the jack of spades. It is usually correct to cover the second honour led in this kind of situation, particularly if you do not have the ten (although with the ten as here, it is unlikely to cost). West played low with fatal results. South exited with the seven of clubs and West was now in deep trouble. The queen of diamonds might have set declarer on the wrong track but, in practice, West played another club, dummy discarding a spade while declarer ruffed. Now she ran the ten of diamonds round to the jack and ruffed the club return, West discarding a spade. She then cashed the ace of spades and, when West played the ten, the count was virtually complete and declarer could enjoy the rest of the diamonds. The overtrick scored well above average as several declarers, sitting North, were held to ten tricks on East's lead of the ten of clubs.

Low cards can be very informative when they are thrown away. On the following hand, the declarer took full advantage of two revealing discards. At teams-of-four, South dealt with North–South vulnerable.

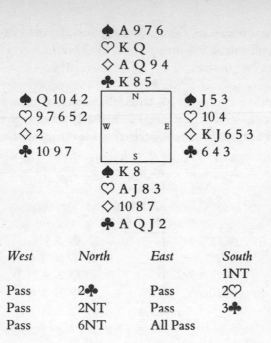

♠ A 9 7 6
♡ K Q
♢ A Q 9 4
♣ K 8 5

♠ Q 10 4 2
♡ 9 7 6 5 2
♢ 2
♣ 10 9 7

N
W   E
S

♠ J 5 3
♡ 10 4
♢ K J 6 5 3
♣ 6 4 3

♠ K 8
♡ A J 8 3
♢ 10 8 7
♣ A Q J 2

West	North	East	South
			1NT
Pass	2♣	Pass	2♡
Pass	2NT	Pass	3♣
Pass	6NT	All Pass	

Two top American ladies were sitting North–South. The opening bid showed 15–17 and after the Stayman inquiry and the two-heart response, two no-trumps was forcing. South showed her second suit and North settled for the no-trump slam. West had little reason to lead a diamond, which would have beaten the contract outright. Instead her choice was the ten of clubs. This was won in dummy and the two heart honours were unblocked. Now South was re-entered with the ace of clubs and two more hearts were cashed, dummy discarding a spade while East discarded two low diamonds. These suggested an original five-card or longer holding and now the hand could be played as an open book. South cashed two more clubs, all following to the first round and all pitching spades on the second. Two top spades, ending in hand, were followed by a low diamond towards the nine in dummy, leaving East to play back the suit round to dummy's tenace. Had East kept three

27

spades and released a third diamond, South would have ducked an early diamond and dropped the king on the second round to promote the queen.

Still on the subject of low cards, the next deal shows that little things mean a lot. The trump suit in this hand seemed nothing to shout about but the female declarer made the most of it.

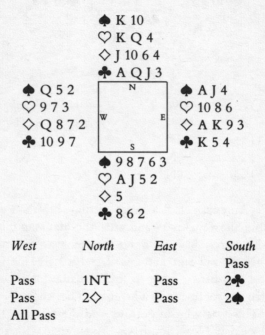

♠ K 10
♡ K Q 4
◇ J 10 6 4
♣ A Q J 3

♠ Q 5 2
♡ 9 7 3
◇ Q 8 7 2
♣ 10 9 7

♠ A J 4
♡ 10 8 6
◇ A K 9 3
♣ K 5 4

♠ 9 8 7 6 3
♡ A J 5 2
◇ 5
♣ 8 6 2

West	North	East	South
			Pass
Pass	1NT	Pass	2♣
Pass	2◇	Pass	2♠
All Pass			

South dealt at Game All in a Swiss teams' event and after two passes, her partner opened one no-trump (14–16). East–West did not enter the bidding and, after a Stayman inquiry proved fruitless, South settled for two spades.

West led the ten of clubs and the queen lost to the king. East switched to top diamonds, South ruffing the second round. Now a trump went to the king and ace and East forced South to ruff a further diamond. Shortened to the same trump length as

28

her opponents, South had no option but to call for more medicine! She crossed to dummy in hearts and ruffed her fourth diamond before exiting in trumps. East won and returned a heart. South cashed her heart and club winners, leaving the defenders to win the last trick in crushing style! Notice that, if the defenders draw trumps after winning the first round, South still has one trump remaining and the clubs and hearts will all score.

5

Perusing the Tabloids

It was mentioned earlier that, for some women, the social aspects of bridge are an important part of their game. It could be argued that this is hardly going to improve performance at the table. However, the ability to listen to the opponents' bidding can earn fabulous rewards, as the next example illustrates. Here the defender was given a choice of ways to surrender.

♠ K J
♡ A K 10 9 5
♢ A 10 7 6
♣ 9 4

♠ 9 8 6 5
♡ J
♢ K J 9
♣ A Q 8 3 2

♠ 7 3
♡ 8 7 3 2
♢ 8 5 4 2
♣ J 7 6

♠ A Q 10 4 2
♡ Q 6 4
♢ Q 3
♣ K 10 5

West	North	East	South
			1♠
2♣	2♡	Pass	4♡
Pass	4♠	Pass	6♠
All Pass			

Modern bidding styles encourage 'getting in' at all costs. This can be particularly dangerous, however, in the presence of an attentive woman. Here West paid heavily for coming in at the two-level on a broken five-card suit, which is unwise at the best of times and particularly so when vulnerable.

In a big pairs event, South dealt at Game All and opened one spade. West overcalled with two clubs and North jumped to three hearts. South raised to four hearts and now North did well to show her spade feature with four spades. That was all South needed; in order to protect her club holding, she bid six spades. This had a chance while six hearts was comfortably beaten at a number of other tables on a minor-suit lead from East.

West's bidding had marked him with most of the outstanding honours and South played the hand double-dummy. She won the opening heart lead in dummy, cashed the king of spades, overtook the jack of spades and ran the rest of the trumps (otherwise West would have an idle card in the endgame) before running the heart suit, keeping the king of clubs and the original ◇Q-3. On the last heart, West was reduced to ♣A-Q and ◇K-J and had the choice of coming down to the blank ace of clubs plus ◇K-J, after which he could be endplayed with the club, or blanking the king of diamonds to allow South two diamond tricks. South read the position perfectly to land the contract.

The best line of defence, which might well have been successful, would be for West to wait until South started cashing dummy's hearts and then discard both the queen of clubs (East keeping the jack) and jack of diamonds early, trying to give the impression of 'blanking' the king. South might then have placed him with six clubs to the A-Q-J and K-J doubleton in diamonds – surely more reasonable on the bidding!

This is the first visit to the spheres of endplay and squeeze but while the defender had two routes to doom, in the next example, there was even the availability of a third option.

In an international team–of–four match, South dealt, vulnerable against non–vulnerable opponents.

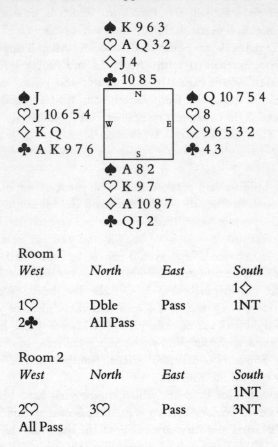

♠ K 9 6 3
♡ A Q 3 2
◇ J 4
♣ 10 8 5

♠ J
♡ J 10 6 5 4
◇ K Q
♣ A K 9 7 6

♠ Q 10 7 5 4
♡ 8
◇ 9 6 5 3 2
♣ 4 3

♠ A 8 2
♡ K 9 7
◇ A 10 8 7
♣ Q J 2

Room 1

West	North	East	South
			1◇
1♡	Dble	Pass	1NT
2♣	All Pass		

Room 2

West	North	East	South
			1NT
2♡	3♡	Pass	3NT
All Pass			

In one room, both the bidding and the play left something to be desired. South, who was playing a strong no–trump in this position, opened one diamond and West overcalled one heart. North doubled, negatively, trying to find a spade fit, and when East passed South could do little but respond one no–trump. West held a very respectable hand and, particularly non–

vulnerable, decided to compete for the part-score by bidding two clubs. He had picked a bad moment. While it is true that his bid is a little dangerous, since his opponents probably have the balance of high-card points and have not established a fit, he does not know that his opponents are intending to play in one no-trump, a contract against which he has fair defensive prospects. Were he to pass and North, say, bid two diamonds, he would be poorly placed to compete on the next round.

As it was, he found his partner with a very unsuitable hand and was lucky that two clubs was passed out. There must surely be a question mark against North for failing to double. This is the sort of situation where doubling can gain a great deal while costing little if the contract is made. North then compounded it by leading the jack of diamonds. Surely her heart holding and her partner's bidding indicated that East was desperately short – almost certainly singleton or void – and a trump lead was indicated. This mistake, however, went unpunished as South was able to win and switch to a trump, holding declarer to four tricks in that suit plus a diamond honour for –150.

There was better play in the other room. South opened one no-trump (14–16) and West came in with two hearts, showing at least nine cards in hearts and a minor. North's bid of three hearts was Lebensohl, promising a heart stopper and a four-card spade suit, thus offering three no-trumps or four spades. South bid three no-trumps and all passed. Again, the opening lead is worthy of discussion. Clearly it had to be a club, but which one? With a certain side entry in diamonds, West decided to play clubs from the top and this gave declarer her chance. South won the third round in hand and played a spade to the king, noticing West's jack. Now came the three of spades from the dummy and, when East played low, South paused to take stock. West's line of defence indicated the two diamond honours, making that jack a likely singleton, so she put in the eight of spades, which held, West being able to spare a heart. Now the ace of spades put the jaws of a triple strip-squeeze on West. She could not spare a red card so she had to take the third option of parting with a winning club. South now ducked a diamond, allowing West to make her last club but no more as the king of diamonds was dropping.

Note that, if East splits his honours, South still prevails. She wins and plays a third spade, catching West as before, while setting up the fourth spade in dummy. West, indeed, had to start with a low club so that communication with her partner would be maintained. Now East does split his honours on the second round of spades and South is helpless. Winning the first club and returning the suit immediately doesn't help either. West cashes her four tricks and exits with a diamond honour and two rounds of spades do not hurt her.

It is, of course, insufficient merely to pay attention at the table. In this next example, the female declarer took full advantage of the information in the bidding and opening lead to avoid trouble.

In a pairs contest, West dealt at Game All.

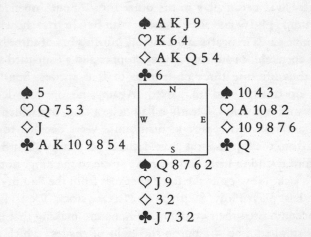

♠ A K J 9
♡ K 6 4
♢ A K Q 5 4
♣ 6

♠ 5
♡ Q 7 5 3
♢ J
♣ A K 10 9 8 5 4

♠ 10 4 3
♡ A 10 8 2
♢ 10 9 8 7 6
♣ Q

♠ Q 8 7 6 2
♡ J 9
♢ 3 2
♣ J 7 3 2

West	North	East	South
3♣	Dble	Pass	3♠
Pass	4♣	Pass	4♠
All Pass			

Despite the presence of a four-card major suit which, for many people, would have precluded a pre-emptive bid in first or second position, West decided to open three clubs. North doubled for take-out and when East passed, South responded with three spades. West passed and North made the cue-bid of four clubs, intending to support spades afterwards to show mild slam ambitions. South could do little but repeat her spades and four spades became the final contract.

West led the jack of diamonds and the failure to lead clubs suggested to South that this might be a singleton. Accordingly, she won in dummy and took two rounds of trumps, to be sure of exhausting West, before playing the six of clubs from dummy. East's queen won and a trump was returned to restrict the club ruffs further. South cashed two more diamonds, discarding a club, and then a fourth round, ruffing in hand. There followed a club ruff in dummy and the last diamond to East's ten which was allowed to hold, South discarding her last club. Left with nothing but hearts, East had to allow the king to score declarer's tenth trick.

As the cards lie, of course, South can succeed by taking just one round of trumps, discarding a heart on the second round of diamonds and then starting on clubs or even by starting on clubs immediately, allowing the diamond ruff, but both lines would have failed if West had started with:

♠ x x   ♡ x x x   ◇ J   ♣ A K x x x x x

more likely, if anything, on the bidding.

6

Uncharted Waters

Sometimes there is little or no information to be gleaned from the bidding and opening lead. It is often necessary for declarer to find out more about a hand for herself, before making a key play. However, women are just as capable as men of doing a little research.

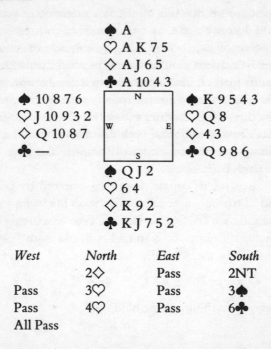

```
                    ♠ A
                    ♡ A K 7 5
                    ◇ A J 6 5
                    ♣ A 10 4 3
    ♠ 10 8 7 6              ♠ K 9 5 4 3
    ♡ J 10 9 3 2           ♡ Q 8
    ◇ Q 10 8 7            ◇ 4 3
    ♣ —                    ♣ Q 9 8 6
                    ♠ Q J 2
                    ♡ 6 4
                    ◇ K 9 2
                    ♣ K J 7 5 2
```

West	North	East	South
	2◇	Pass	2NT
Pass	3♡	Pass	3♠
Pass	4♡	Pass	6♣
All Pass			

On this occasion, North dealt at Game All in a team-of-four

match. Her opening bid of two diamonds showed a strong hand with a 4–4–4–1 shape, the singleton as yet unspecified. The opposition were silent throughout and South's response of two no-trumps was a relay, asking her partner to specify the singleton. North showed her singleton spade by bidding three hearts, and South bid three spades, conventionally asking for controls. North's reply of four hearts showed nine controls, counting an ace as two and a king as one. That was enough for South to bid the small slam in clubs.

West led the jack of hearts and South realized that much depended on the trump situation. Winning in dummy with the ace, she decided that it was wise to try and learn more about the hand, notably who had the length in hearts. For that reason, she immediately played the king of hearts, and when East dropped the queen, it seemed likely that, if anyone was long in clubs, it would be East and therefore that the queen was more likely to be found in that hand. Accordingly, she cashed the ace of clubs and, when West showed out, all was revealed. The South hand was now an entry short to take the diamond finesse and the two spade ruffs which were needed for the contract. However, the declarer worked on an endgame involving only one ruff. She took the marked trump finesse, cashed a third round, crossed to the ace of spades and returned to the king of diamonds for the diamond finesse. That left:

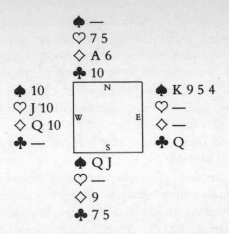

```
                ♠ —
                ♡ 7 5
                ◇ A 6
                ♣ 10
    ♠ 10          ┌──────────┐      ♠ K 9 5 4
    ♡ J 10        │    N     │      ♡ —
    ◇ Q 10        │ W      E │      ◇ —
    ♣ —           │    S     │      ♣ Q
                  └──────────┘
                ♠ Q J
                ♡ —
                ◇ 9
                ♣ 7 5
```

Now the ace of diamonds left East without resource. If she ruffed, she would have to lead a spade, setting up an extra trick in the suit for South, whoever held the king. If she did not, South would simply carry on a crossruff, leaving East to play the queen of clubs any time she liked.

This was a beautiful endplay but it has to said there is a simpler line by which South can, after all, take her two spade ruffs. After the trump ace reveals the break, South cashes the ace of spades, plays a diamond to the king, takes the diamond finesse, takes a trump finesse and ruffs a spade. Now a heart from dummy forces East to discard a spade (ruffing does not help), South ruffs in hand and ruffs another spade. Now the ace of diamonds is ruffed by East but South is waiting with two more trumps at the end.

In the previous example, because the necessary key play was in the trump suit, declarer could do only a limited amount of research before making a decision. When the crucial guess is in a side-suit, declarer can usually discover even more about the hand.

At teams-of-four, North dealt at Game All.

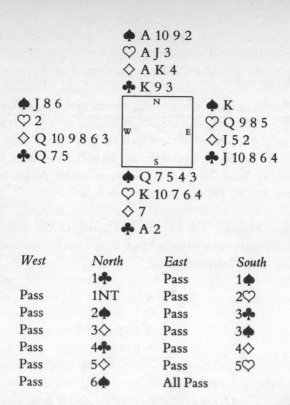

♠ A 10 9 2
♡ A J 3
◇ A K 4
♣ K 9 3

♠ J 8 6
♡ 2
◇ Q 10 9 8 6 3
♣ Q 7 5

♠ K
♡ Q 9 8 5
◇ J 5 2
♣ J 10 8 6 4

♠ Q 7 5 4 3
♡ K 10 7 6 4
◇ 7
♣ A 2

West	North	East	South
	1♣	Pass	1♠
Pass	1NT	Pass	2♡
Pass	2♠	Pass	3♣
Pass	3◇	Pass	3♠
Pass	4♣	Pass	4◇
Pass	5◇	Pass	5♡
Pass	6♠	All Pass	

She opened a strong one club. With East–West silent, South bid
a natural one spade, showing at least eight points and five or
more spades. North bid one no-trump and South two hearts.
North gave preference to spades and, after a long series of
cue-bids. South finished in six spades.

West had listened to the bidding and avoided the fatal heart
lead in favour of the ten of diamonds to dummy's ace. There are
a number of ways to play the trump suit but as South wanted to
hold the lead with a view to a possible elimination of the minors
and throw-in to avoid that heart guess, she started with the ace,
felling East's king. It appeared that the minor suits could be
stripped and West thrown in with the third round of trumps to
open up the hearts or give a ruff and discard.

That line, however, appears to fail because South will have run out of trumps. But – never mind – the declarer just carried on, regardless of such a piffling consideration. She played the ace of diamonds and ruffed the last one in hand. There followed three rounds of clubs, also ruffing the last one in hand and then the queen and another spade. West 'safely' exited with a fourth round of diamonds but, when East showed out, West could be counted for six diamonds, three spades and three clubs, leaving, at most, one heart. Thus after the ace of hearts, South was able to finesse the ten, fully confident of success.

This next example shows an application of the principle of restricted choice. In a pairs contest, South dealt, non-vulnerable against vulnerable opponents.

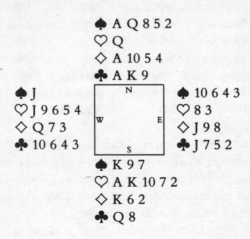

♠ A Q 8 5 2
♡ Q
♢ A 10 5 4
♣ A K 9

♠ J
♡ J 9 6 5 4
♢ Q 7 3
♣ 10 6 4 3

♠ 10 6 4 3
♡ 8 3
♢ J 9 8
♣ J 7 5 2

♠ K 9 7
♡ A K 10 7 2
♢ K 6 2
♣ Q 8

West	North	East	South
			1♡
Pass	1♠	Pass	1NT
Pass	3♢	Pass	4♠
Pass	5♣	Pass	5♡
Pass	6♣	Pass	6♢
Pass	7NT	All Pass	

She opened one heart and with East–West silent throughout, North replied with one spade; South rebid one no-trump and when North jumped to three diamonds, South showed her suitability with a jump to four spades. Cue-bidding followed and, because of the method of scoring, North tried for seven no-trumps.

West led the three of clubs, won by South's queen. Declarer continued with the nine of spades, noting the fall of West's jack. At this stage, it could have been singleton or a doubleton or trebleton with the ten. Now the queen of hearts was cashed and the closed hand re-entered with the king of diamonds for two more rounds of hearts, revealing the distribution in that suit. A woman's refusal to be hurried paid dividends here in that the declarer had thus delayed the critical guess until she had accumulated as much information as possible. The odds now favoured a restricted choice finesse against East's ten of spades, so she crossed to dummy in clubs and played a low spade, putting in the seven when East played low. After that, she cashed the king and returned to dummy with the ace of diamonds to enjoy the rest of the spades for a top.

7

Panorama

Much has already been said about attention to detail, but women are also capable of taking a broader view of matters when the situation demands. This is particularly applicable in the circumstances of the following example.

The importance of considering the whole hand rather than making the 'technically correct' play in a single suit was well illustrated in this deal from a match between teams of four from the Houses of Parliament and their Swedish counterparts, played with aggregate scoring.

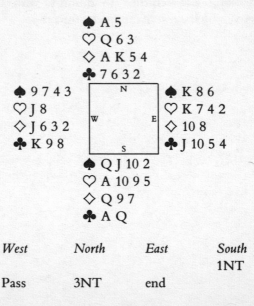

```
              ♠ A 5
              ♡ Q 6 3
              ◇ A K 5 4
              ♣ 7 6 3 2
  ♠ 9 7 4 3       N        ♠ K 8 6
  ♡ J 8                    ♡ K 7 4 2
  ◇ J 6 3 2   W       E    ◇ 10 8
  ♣ K 9 8                  ♣ J 10 5 4
                  S
              ♠ Q J 10 2
              ♡ A 10 9 5
              ◇ Q 9 7
              ♣ A Q
```

West	North	East	South
			1NT
Pass	3NT	end	

In both rooms, South dealt at Game All and opened one no-trump (15–17) which North raised to game. When a Swedish man sat South, West led the three of spades and the declarer observed the usual rule of second-hand-low, happy to have a free finesse or the whole suit set up should East be able to win. Actually, East produced the king and switched to a low club. South tried the finesse but that also lost and the ace was knocked out. Declarer now tried the diamonds and, when they failed to break, led the queen of hearts from dummy. East covered and, when the jack did not fall, the contract was defeated.

Even after the early mishaps, South could have saved himself. Instead of touching hearts, he should exit with a club. The defenders can cash two tricks in clubs or (better) cash one trick in clubs and one in diamonds. In the first case, East has to lead away from his king of hearts and South cannot go wrong. In the second, West has to lead hearts and South must guess well.

But now observe what happened when a woman was sitting South for the British in the other room. She also received the spade lead but, to avoid embarrassment in clubs, she won immediately in dummy and played a heart to the ten and West's jack. West could not profitably attack clubs from his side and now the declarer had time to set up enough tricks in the majors.

This hand illustrates the necessity of considering the hand as a whole, rather than just playing suit combinations in isolation. It is the defenders' task to divert declarer down the wrong path.

Sitting South at teams-of-four, you open a 15–17 one no-trump at Game All. Partner raises you to three no-trumps and the woman sitting West, playing normal fourth-highest leads, starts with the five of hearts.

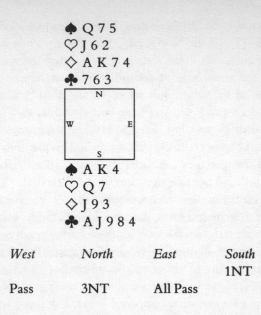

♠ Q 7 5
♡ J 6 2
◇ A K 7 4
♣ 7 6 3

♠ A K 4
♡ Q 7
◇ J 9 3
♣ A J 9 8 4

West	North	East	South
			1NT
Pass	3NT	All Pass	

East takes the trick with her ace and returns the ten to West's king. West persists with the three of hearts and dummy's jack wins, East discarding a low spade. How do you continue?

The correct line of play in the club suit would normally be small to the nine, hoping to find East with one top honour together with the ten. However, on this deal, that would lead to immediate defeat for West would then be able to cash all his heart tricks. Prospects look poor and it appears that you will need to find East with both club honours, but you could afford to cash the ace first in case West has one of them singleton. There is, however, one small additional chance. If West has a singleton queen of diamonds, you could set up four tricks in that suit through a marked finesse against East's ten. That means you will need only one club trick. Superb analysis – so you play the ace of diamonds and your efforts are justly rewarded when West produces the queen. Well played! You can now take the marked finesse against East's ten, and the result? Two off in a stone-cold contract. This was the full deal:

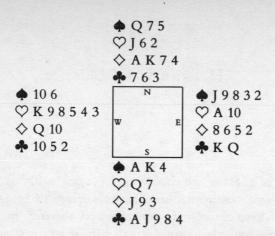

```
                  ♠ Q 7 5
                  ♡ J 6 2
                  ◇ A K 7 4
                  ♣ 7 6 3
   ♠ 10 6              N           ♠ J 9 8 3 2
   ♡ K 9 8 5 4 3                  ♡ A 10
   ◇ Q 10        W        E       ◇ 8 6 5 2
   ♣ 10 5 2                       ♣ K Q
                     S
                  ♠ A K 4
                  ♡ Q 7
                  ◇ J 9 3
                  ♣ A J 9 8 4
```

While you were thinking the hand out, so was West! She could see that her best hope of an entry was the ten of diamonds, and her only chance was to convince you that she didn't hold it.

8

Harmony and Balance

Bridge is a game which involves playing with one partner against two opponents, and the importance of being able to strike a balance between consideration towards partner and toughness towards opponents can hardly be overemphasized. The next few examples illustrate the woman's uncanny ability to discriminate in this respect. The feminine propensity for caring for others emerges especially in defensive signalling.

On the following hand, one woman made sure that her partner (actually her husband) took the right view here with a defence which recent jargon describes as a 'foghorn'.

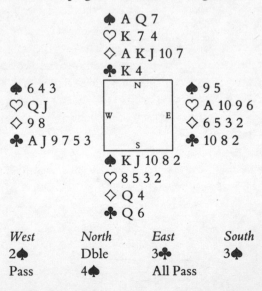

♠ A Q 7
♥ K 7 4
♦ A K J 10 7
♣ K 4

♠ 6 4 3
♥ Q J
♦ 9 8
♣ A J 9 7 5 3

♠ 9 5
♥ A 10 9 6
♦ 6 5 3 2
♣ 10 8 2

♠ K J 10 8 2
♥ 8 5 3 2
♦ Q 4
♣ Q 6

West	North	East	South
2♣	Dble	3♣	3♠
Pass	4♠	All Pass	

In a mixed-teams event, our heroine was sitting West and opened two spades. This is one of those modern two-way two-bids which, on this occasion, showed an Acol two in spades or a weak pre-empt in clubs. North doubled, showing general values, and East corrected to three clubs, prepared to play in three spades should his partner turn out to have a strong two in that suit. As it was, South bid three spades and North raised to four spades.

It was difficult for North–South to reached the laydown three no-trumps, because of their opponents' pre-emptive bidding.

West led the queen of hearts. South can make the contract if he covers because then the suit is blocked. However, in view of the club length, he not unreasonably took the view that this was more likely to be a singleton and decided to play low to the trick. East encouraged with the ten and, when the queen held the trick, West carefully paused to consider. A thoughtless defender would have calmly persisted with the jack of hearts, but then what is East to do when South plays low again? Anything could be right. To keep her partner on the right track, West cashed the ace of clubs and only then played the jack of hearts. The apparently unnecessary cashing of a winner (usually an ace) in situations of this kind indicates to partner that the following card is (now) a singleton. East was thus able to overtake confidently and give his partner a ruff for the setting trick. Note that, if the jack of hearts is allowed to hold, East–West cannot enjoy their third heart trick, the enemy taking ten tricks in spades and diamonds first.

Situations of this kind occur frequently and are mishandled all too often. Here is another example:

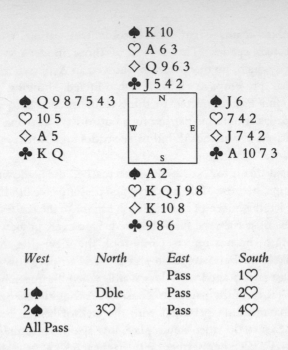

♠ K 10
♡ A 6 3
♢ Q 9 6 3
♣ J 5 4 2

♠ Q 9 8 7 5 4 3
♡ 10 5
♢ A 5
♣ K Q

N
W E
S

♠ J 6
♡ 7 4 2
♢ J 7 4 2
♣ A 10 7 3

♠ A 2
♡ K Q J 9 8
♢ K 10 8
♣ 9 8 6

West	North	East	South
		Pass	1♡
1♠	Dble	Pass	2♡
2♠	3♡	Pass	4♡
All Pass			

Women were sitting North–South against male opposition in a pairs contest. At Love All, East dealt and passed; South opened one heart and West overcalled with one spade. North made a negative double and, when East passed again, South bid two hearts. West competed with two spades and, when North raised to three hearts, South pushed on to game.

West led the seven of spades, which South won in hand, played a low diamond to the queen and ducked a diamond. Now West should have cashed his clubs, but instead tried to give his partner a spade ruff. He might have asked himself why there was no attempt to draw trumps; also East had contributed very low diamonds to both rounds played.

However, as the play went, declarer was able to pounce. She won the king of spades and cashed exactly two rounds of trumps in hand to leave these cards still outstanding:

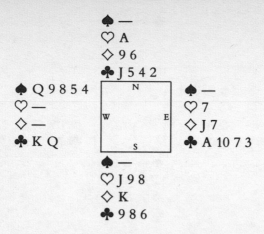

```
                    ♠ —
                    ♡ A
                    ◇ 9 6
                    ♣ J 5 4 2
♠ Q 9 8 5 4      ┌──────────┐      ♠ —
♡ —              │    N     │      ♡ 7
◇ —              │ W      E │      ◇ J 7
♣ K Q            │    S     │      ♣ A 10 7 3
                 └──────────┘
                    ♠ —
                    ♡ J 9 8
                    ◇ K
                    ♣ 9 8 6
```

She now cashed the king of diamonds and exited in clubs. West cashed his two honours but on the second round the defence was in a cleft stick. If the king was allowed to hold, West would have to concede a ruff and discard, saving South the third club loser. If East overtook, the jack would become declarer's tenth trick.

Strangely, this board proved little better than average as there was an alternative road to stardom. At a number of other tables, West did indeed cash his clubs at tricks one and two, ruling out the endplay. This time the spade switch was won in dummy and three rounds of trumps taken, again ending in dummy. Now a diamond was played to the ten and West's ace (if he ducks, South must continue with the king of diamonds). West exited in spades but South was able to win in hand and cash two more trumps. This was the position as the last one was led:

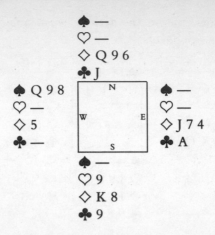

```
              ♠ —
              ♡ —
              ◇ Q 9 6
              ♣ J
  ♠ Q 9 8   ┌─────────┐   ♠ —
  ♡ —       │    N    │   ♡ —
  ◇ 5       │ W     E │   ◇ J 7 4
  ♣ —       │    S    │   ♣ A
            └─────────┘
              ♠ —
              ♡ 9
              ◇ K 8
              ♣ 9
```

West discarded a spade and dummy the jack of clubs but East
was left without resource.

Possibly a pair playing Roman leads would have found the
defence to break the contract. West leads the king and queen of
clubs and, as on that lead system, this is the 'wrong way round',
East will be aware of the doubleton and overtake to give his
partner a club ruff. Now the ace of diamonds becomes the
defenders' fourth trick. Playing normal leads, another foghorn
signal is required. West leads the king of clubs and, when his
partner encourages (clearly indicting the ace as the jack is visible
in dummy), he now cashes the ace of diamonds, the foghorn to
indicate that the next lead will be a singleton, and only then
plays the queen of clubs; East should now realize what is going
on. That aside, provided declarer plays at least two rounds of
trumps before touching diamonds, starting with a low card
towards the ten and intending to continue with the king to avoid
blocking the suit, it appears that declarer will prevail.

The need for correct timing in defence is illustrated again here
when a woman took careful note of her partner's (again her
husband's) signalling to ensure that the defence was timed per-

fectly. In a pairs contest, she dealt as West, vulnerable against non-vulnerable opponents.

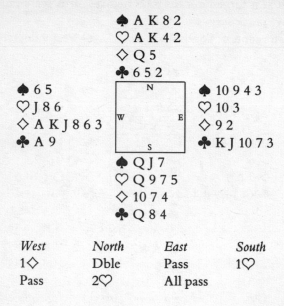

♠ A K 8 2
♡ A K 4 2
◇ Q 5
♣ 6 5 2

♠ 6 5
♡ J 8 6
◇ A K J 8 6 3
♣ A 9

♠ 10 9 4 3
♡ 10 3
◇ 9 2
♣ K J 10 7 3

♠ Q J 7
♡ Q 9 7 5
◇ 10 7 4
♣ Q 8 4

West	North	East	South
1◇	Dble	Pass	1♡
Pass	2♡	All pass	

West opened one diamond, North doubled, East passed and South bid one heart. West passed and North raised to two hearts which became the final contract.

West led three top diamonds and, when East petered, South discarded a club from dummy on the third round, East taking the opportunity to signal with the jack of clubs. Accordingly, West underled the ace of clubs to her partner's king and only after the second round to the ace was the time ripe to play a fourth diamond, forcing a trump promotion while South had no more losers to discard. West's trumps were just good enough after East's ten had forced South's queen. It was certainly a very close-run affair, as we need only exchange the positions of the five and six of hearts and the contract can still be made if South reads the trump layout correctly.

Care for partner is not, of course, confined to defence. In this next example, a woman helped her partner in the bidding, although as it turned out his intermediate cards were purely for decorative purposes.

In a pairs contest, South dealt, with East–West vulnerable.

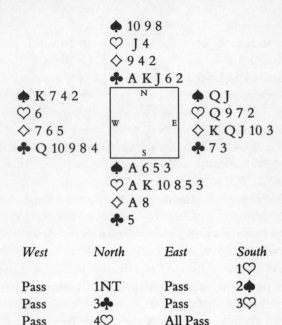

♠ 10 9 8
♡ J 4
♢ 9 4 2
♣ A K J 6 2

♠ K 7 4 2
♡ 6
♢ 7 6 5
♣ Q 10 9 8 4

♠ Q J
♡ Q 9 7 2
♢ K Q J 10 3
♣ 7 3

♠ A 6 5 3
♡ A K 10 8 5 3
♢ A 8
♣ 5

West	North	East	South
			1♡
Pass	1NT	Pass	2♠
Pass	3♣	Pass	3♡
Pass	4♡	All Pass	

The dealer opened one heart and, with East–West silent throughout, North responded with one no-trump. South now made the descriptive bid of two spades. This forcing reverse gave a more accurate description of her hand than a direct three hearts. North showed his values with three clubs and, when South bid three hearts, he raised to game, hoping that his spade intermediates would be of some value. In practice, they were worth no more than a refrigerator to an eskimo, but that was not his fault!

Despite the bidding, West led the two of spades and, as the fourth round of the suit would be lost to West's seven, South realized that she had to work on it immediately. Accordingly, she played low at trick one, won the diamond return, cashed two top clubs, discarding her losing diamond, and played ace and another spade. She was thus able to ruff the fourth round with the jack and, if East refused to overruff, a finesse of the ten of hearts would ensure that only one trump trick was lost. East actually did overruff but that was the last trick for the defence.

The defenders might have made life more difficult had they attacked trumps at trick two but now, even if declarer misreads the position in that suit, she is forced into the club finesse, which holds, so that her third losing spade can be discarded. Thus she should never lose more than two tricks in spades and one in trumps.

9

The Crystal Ball

In life as a whole, women are generally good at planning and looking ahead to possible future problems – even if at times that skill is confined only to organizing dinner parties! This ability stands them in good stead at the bridge table and the next example demonstrates the reward.

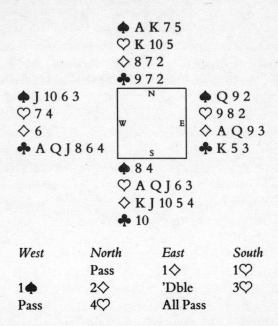

	♠ A K 7 5	
	♡ K 10 5	
	♢ 8 7 2	
	♣ 9 7 2	
♠ J 10 6 3		♠ Q 9 2
♡ 7 4		♡ 9 8 2
♢ 6		♢ A Q 9 3
♣ A Q J 8 6 4		♣ K 5 3
	♠ 8 4	
	♡ A Q J 6 3	
	♢ K J 10 5 4	
	♣ 10	

West	North	East	South
	Pass	1♢	1♡
1♠	2♢	'Dble	3♡
Pass	4♡	All Pass	

This hand came up in a women's world championship final of a few years back. North dealt, vulnerable against non-vulnerable opponents and passed. East, playing a five-card major system, opened one diamond and South overcalled with one heart. West bid one spade and North made the cue-bid of two diamonds, requesting more information from partner. East doubled to show three-card spade support – a commonly played convention in North America – and South jumped to three hearts, which North raised to game.

In one room, East–West were very keen on the foghorn principle, which has already been illustrated a number of times: if one cashes an ace and then switches, the switch card will be a singleton. Accordingly, she cashed the ace of clubs and switched to the diamond, duly collecting the ruff but no more, to concede 620.

In the other room, West appreciated that an entry might be needed to her partner's hand and led the diamond at trick one. East won and returned the three of diamonds as a suit preference for clubs. West ruffed and duly underled her ace of clubs to receive a second ruff and +100.

To be realistic, it should be pointed out that both Wests missed the opportunity to pick the right foghorn. Surely with eight high-card points, including an ace, and a singleton in partner's suit, they should have doubled the final contract. There would have been little risk of a redouble and/or overtricks and this would have made the diamond position clear. Now the ace of clubs lead would not have been necessary.

Unselfishness at the bridge table is always thought to be directed at partner. The female bridge player seems to know when to appear to be 'kind' to opponents. This next hand gives an excellent example of an unwanted gift. Beginners are taught never to give away a ruff and discard. Often women know when it is fitting to bestow this kind of generosity!

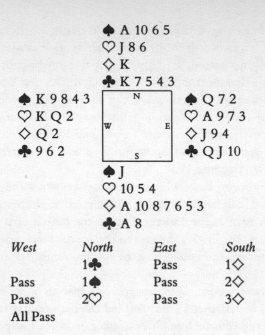

♠ A 10 6 5
♡ J 8 6
◇ K
♣ K 7 5 4 3

♠ K 9 8 4 3
♡ K Q 2
◇ Q 2
♣ 9 6 2

♠ Q 7 2
♡ A 9 7 3
◇ J 9 4
♣ Q J 10

♠ J
♡ 10 5 4
◇ A 10 8 7 6 5 3
♣ A 8

West	North	East	South
	1♣	Pass	1◇
Pass	1♠	Pass	2◇
Pass	2♡	Pass	3◇
All Pass			

At teams-of-four, North dealt at Love All and two men sitting North–South bid against silent female opposition. North opened one club, South bid one diamond, North one spade and South two diamonds. At this point, North might well have been advised to give up the argument, but male stubbornness predominated and he tried for no-trumps with a fourth-suit-forcing bid of two hearts. South felt he could do nothing but repeat his diamonds and bought the contract in three diamonds.

The heart lead stood out and the woman sitting West started with the king. When East encouraged with the seven, she continued with the queen and a third round to East's ace. At this point, East realized that a ruff and discard could well gain in promoting her jack of trumps and would certainly not do worse than break even, even if South could discard a black-suit loser, so she played her last heart. South ruffed low but West tossed in her queen of trumps, forcing North's king. South could not now avoid losing two trump tricks to East, and the contract.

10

Accepting Limitations

Of course, women, just like men, are human beings and therefore fallible. Sometimes it is difficult to be sufficiently far-sighted to cater for every eventuality, and although the declarer on our next deal made a contract in which her male counterpart failed, she did make a significant slip early in the play. However, it would have taken an extremely alert defender of either sex to force her to pay for this error.

With two women at the table having apparently gone wrong at some stage, this hand might arguably have been more suitable for Joyce Nicholson's book. However, a detailed analysis is given here as it contains an excellent example of the use of card-reading and a number of other instructive points. It therefore will repay careful study.

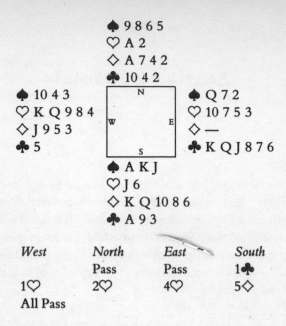

```
              ♠ 9 8 6 5
              ♡ A 2
              ◇ A 7 4 2
              ♣ 10 4 2
♠ 10 4 3          N          ♠ Q 7 2
♡ K Q 9 8 4              ♡ 10 7 5 3
◇ J 9 5 3    W       E    ◇ —
♣ 5                        ♣ K Q J 8 7 6
                 S
              ♠ A K J
              ♡ J 6
              ◇ K Q 10 8 6
              ♣ A 9 3
```

West	North	East	South
	Pass	Pass	1♣
1♡	2♡	4♡	5◇
All Pass			

In an international team-of-four match, North dealt at Love All and, after two passes, South, paying a strong one-club system, opened one club. West overcalled with one heart and North's cue-bid showed eight points or more without length or strength in hearts. East bounced to four hearts but South refused to be barraged and bought the contract in five diamonds. West led the king of hearts. Now – would you like to put your money down? On best play all round, should declarer or defenders prevail?

At the table, South won the lead in dummy and played a low diamond to her king, the bad news being revealed when East discarded a club. South now cashed the ace of spades and led the eight of diamonds, covered by the nine and ace. A successful spade finesse was followed by the king of spades and, when all followed, West was known to have five hearts, four diamonds and three spades, leaving one club – and it was this club shortage that gave declarer her chance. She cashed the ace of clubs and got off play with the jack of hearts to West's queen in this position:

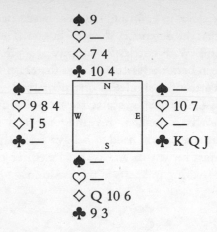

```
              ♠ 9
              ♡ —
              ◇ 7 4
              ♣ 10 4
    ♠ —        ┌─── N ───┐      ♠ —
    ♡ 9 8 4    │          │      ♡ 10 7
    ◇ J 5    W │          │ E    ◇ —
    ♣ —        │          │      ♣ K Q J
              └─── S ───┘
              ♠ —
              ♡ —
              ◇ Q 10 6
              ♣ 9 3
```

West now had three ways of giving declarer the contract:

1 The jack of diamonds allows South to finish the drawing of trumps in dummy and enjoy the spade.
2 A low diamond is won by the seven in dummy, after which the spade is led and a club discarded. The trump trick comes back but now West has to concede a ruff and discard.
3 A heart lead allows South to ruff on dummy, while discarding a club from hand. Now the other club is discarded on the spade and West can take her trump trick whenever she likes.

So it appears declarer has done well to make her contract, but West had an answer. Forgoing her trump trick at trick four by refusing to cover the eight of diamonds, playing the five instead, would have paid handsome dividends. If the eight is allowed to hold, South cannot take the spade finesse and eliminate the suit early enough. If South takes her ace of diamonds immediately, West cannot be endplayed as the ◇J-9 are now solid and South must lose three tricks.

South might try the six of diamonds at trick four instead of the eight but that is no better because now West *does* play the nine. All South's trumps are now high and in the endplay position West can get off play in trumps. Thus South completes the drawing of them in hand and has to concede two club tricks. So it appears that the defenders have it – but no! The real mistake came earlier still. With entries to dummy at a premium, South might have been better advised to forgo the benefit of the small percentage chance of a singleton queen of spades in the West hand and take the spade finesse at trick two. Now, when the king of diamonds is cashed, revealing the bad news, South realizes that the spades will need to behave perfectly and that the distribution must be as it is and cashes her three top black-suit winners before exiting in hearts in this position.

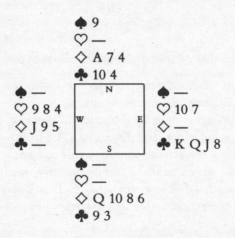

West has had to win the heart trick if the defence is to have any chance, otherwise South plays two more rounds of trumps, ending in dummy and discards a club on the spade, losing only a club and a diamond. But what does she lead now? Any diamond allows South to complete the drawing of trumps on dummy after which she can enjoy the master spade, so West must lead a heart. South ruffs in dummy, discarding a club from hand, and has the choice of playing the spade now, discarding the other club, or playing two rounds of trumps, ending in dummy, and then playing the spade. Either way, she concedes one trick in each red suit but no more.

11

That Good Old Intuition

Current trends in bidding include an aggressive overcalling style, the reasons for which are to make life more difficult for the opposition and to help partner find the winning opening lead. However, sometimes aggressive overcalls are doubled and lose a substantial penalty, and on occasions attention to the bidding can enable the winning opening lead to be found without any help from partner.

In the introduction, the New York–Paris 'battle of the sexes' match was mentioned and this hand did much to advance the women's cause.

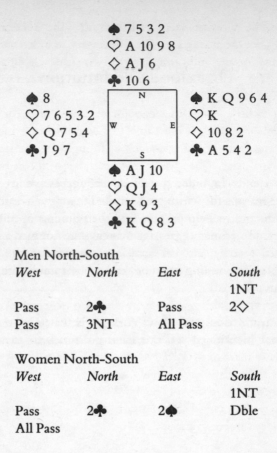

♠ 7 5 3 2
♡ A 10 9 8
♦ A J 6
♣ 10 6

♠ 8
♡ 7 6 5 3 2
♦ Q 7 5 4
♣ J 9 7

♠ K Q 9 6 4
♡ K
♦ 10 8 2
♣ A 5 4 2

♠ A J 10
♡ Q J 4
♦ K 9 3
♣ K Q 8 3

Men North–South

West	North	East	South
			1NT
Pass	2♣	Pass	2♦
Pass	3NT	All Pass	

Women North–South

West	North	East	South
			1NT
Pass	2♣	2♠	Dble
All Pass			

At both tables, South, dealer at Game All, opened one no–trump (15–17). When the men were North–South, East–West were silent throughout and North made a Stayman inquiry. On hearing the bad news, he settled for three no–trumps. West, with her very poor hand, decided that the best chance was to try and find her partner's suit and promptly led her spade to the queen and ace. South took the losing heart finesse, whereupon East cleared the suit and waited for her ace of clubs to take two more spade tricks to defeat the contract.

When the women were North–South, the auction started similarly but the sitting East felt it necessary to indicate the spade lead to his partner and came in with two spades. South doubled and East did well to hold the loss to 800 but the men still lost 14 IMPs.

There is little doubt that enough material exists for a whole book to be written on the subject of lead-directing bids alone, but this case surely indicates lack of thought on the part of the man sitting East. The clue to his best action lies in his point-count; twelve. It implied that, if his opponents reached game in no-trumps, usually requiring around twenty-five or more points, his partner would be unlikely to hold more than about three points and therefore had little prospect of developing his own suit. In such circumstances, it is normal to try to find partner's suit on opening lead, whether or not he has bid.

Furthermore, it always much more dangerous to enter the auction when both opponents are likely to have balanced hands with no particularly good fit. If the opponents do have a fit, it is likely to be in hearts, when there is no guarantee that a spade lead would be crucial or that West would fail to find it anyway. If East's intentions were merely to compete for a part-score, it would have been much safer to wait for the next round, by which time he would know more about his opponents' combined values and distribution.

12

Time for Oneself

Unfortunately the world at large is full of people, both men and women, who seem to take great pleasure in inflicting pain and misery on others. At the bridge table, one is expected to be charming and courteous towards one's opponents at all times, but pain and misery can be inflicted in subtle ways.

In this example, a female declarer broke one of the basic rules of cardplay by choosing to lead away from her honours rather than towards them, and in doing so made life very unpleasant to her opponents.

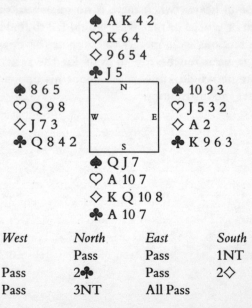

```
                    ♠ A K 4 2
                    ♡ K 6 4
                    ◇ 9 6 5 4
                    ♣ J 5
        ♠ 8 6 5                      ♠ 10 9 3
        ♡ Q 9 8         N            ♡ J 5 3 2
        ◇ J 7 3    W         E       ◇ A 2
        ♣ Q 8 4 2       S            ♣ K 9 6 3
                    ♠ Q J 7
                    ♡ A 10 7
                    ◇ K Q 10 8
                    ♣ A 10 7
```

West	North	East	South
	Pass	Pass	1NT
Pass	2♣	Pass	2◇
Pass	3NT	All Pass	

In a pairs contest, North dealt at Game All. After two passes, South opened one no-trump, showing 15–17 points. With East–West silent, North bid Stayman and, when South failed to produce a major, North settled for three no-trumps.

Playing top-of-nothing leads, West led the eight of spades. South won in hand and cashed her other spade honour before crossing to dummy with a third round. Her first good play was to refrain from cashing the fourth round – she had no convenient discard at this stage. Instead, she attacked diamonds at once, winning the first round with the king. Most players would now have returned to the king of hearts for a second round of diamonds, but our declarer paused to take stock. That opening lead was suspicious. It clearly came from a short suit and, if West held a doubleton diamond only, she would have two four-card suits from which to choose or possibly even a five-card suit. It thus seemed more likely that West held a flat hand and thus, trying to give the impression of an awkward heart holding, declarer was mean enough to play the ten of diamonds from hand, dropping East's ace and at the same time, being generous enough with the rope for East to finish herself.

She had also noticed South's reluctance to play a heart, which suggested a tenace holding. She thus decided that attacking clubs was less dangerous and switched to low one, allowing declarer two tricks in the suit for two overtricks. Other declarers, who played the king of hearts early, were held to ten tricks as a heart switch was now safe. It is instructive to note that, had East considered South's point-count, she might have realized that, with the queen and jack of spades and the king of diamonds already shown, South was likely to have at least seven points in the other two suits and thus, almost certainly, the ace of hearts. Consequently, a heart switch would cost only if South had exactly ♡A-10-9. The club switch would certainly cost if South had the ace and queen or ace and ten. That does not, however, detract from South's play. Defenders will never go wrong unless they are given a chance.

Nevertheless, the unkindness of declarer's diamond play on this hand is nothing compared to that in our next example.

Just imagine yourself, a kindly soul, sitting East in a pairs contest. You pick up your usual rock-crusher:

♠ 9 8 7 3   ♡ J 10   ◇ 9 3   ♣ 9 8 6 3 2

Oh yes – one more point than usual! But there is no cause for complacency. A woman is sitting on your left, and need you be told what is going to happen? Of course, you have guessed already – you are going to be squeezed! Just let the tears roll aimlessly down your cheeks as this tale of ultimate misery unfolds.

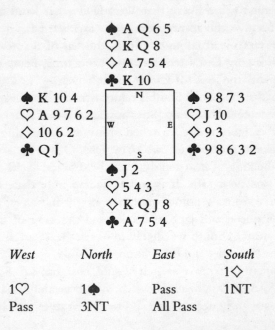

	♠ A Q 6 5	
	♡ K Q 8	
	◇ A 7 5 4	
	♣ K 10	
♠ K 10 4	N	♠ 9 8 7 3
♡ A 9 7 6 2	W E	♡ J 10
◇ 10 6 2	S	◇ 9 3
♣ Q J		♣ 9 8 6 3 2
	♠ J 2	
	♡ 5 4 3	
	◇ K Q J 8	
	♣ A 7 5 4	

West	North	East	South
			1◇
1♡	1♠	Pass	1NT
Pass	3NT	All Pass	

South deals at Love All and opens one diamond. Your partner overcalls with one heart and North bids one spade, which is forcing. You make your usual contribution to the auction and South rebids one no-trump, showing a minimum opener. Partner passes and North raises to three no-trumps, the final contract.

Partner leads the six of hearts to the king, jack and three. Dummy's five of spades goes to the three, jack and partner's king and partner switches to the queen of clubs, won by dummy's king. Now the four of diamonds is taken by South's king and a heart is led. Partner takes the ace and plays the jack of clubs to South's ace. South now cashes the queen of hearts and three more rounds of diamonds. You can spare two clubs but what do you discard on the last round? (It will be a surprise if you get this one right.)

No, you do not discard a spade, because now dummy's spades all hold and South makes eleven tricks. And you do not discard another club, because that sets up South's seven – again eleven tricks. You simply discard your partner! On this occasion, your partner has aided and abetted declarer in her unkindness by carefully rectifying the count when she won her ace of hearts. Ducking would have made ten tricks the limit.

13

Fitting in

Another attribute which is essential to success at the very top in bridge is the ability to be flexible. In the following example, the female declarer appreciated the need to revise her plan of campaign while the male defender failed to do so.

In an international teams-of-four match, East dealt at Game All:

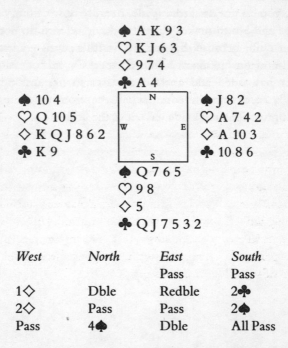

```
              ♠ A K 9 3
              ♡ K J 6 3
              ◇ 9 7 4
              ♣ A 4
♠ 10 4                      ♠ J 8 2
♡ Q 10 5          N        ♡ A 7 4 2
◇ K Q J 8 6 2   W   E      ◇ A 10 3
♣ K 9             S        ♣ 10 8 6
              ♠ Q 7 6 5
              ♡ 9 8
              ◇ 5
              ♣ Q J 7 5 3 2
```

West	North	East	South
		Pass	Pass
1◇	Dble	Redble	2♣
2◇	Pass	Pass	2♠
Pass	4♠	Dble	All Pass

East and South both passed and when West opened one diamond, North doubled and East redoubled to show nine or more points. South bid two clubs and West, with a hand clearly unsuitable for defence (especially opposite a passed partner), repeated his diamonds. This was passed round to South, who reopened with two spades. West passed and North had a late rush of blood. With South having promised a very distributional hand, most if not all his top cards were working and a game invitation was clearly in order. However, not one for half-measure, he bid four spades outright and East doubled. Sadly, his defence was not to prove up to his bidding!

West led the king of diamonds and continued the suit when it held. South ruffed and, realizing that her original hope of enjoying the long clubs had now been dashed, turned her thoughts to a crossruff. She led the queen of clubs to the king and ace and returned the suit to the jack. A third club now would have invited trouble in the form of a trump promotion, so she switched to the eight of hearts. West covered with the ten and dummy played the jack.

At this point, East erred on two counts. First, it is probably better to refuse this trick to cut declarer's communications in the suit, although South can get back to hand by ruffing a diamond. As it was, East won but that wasn't fatal. Even at this point, a trump switch would have made life too difficult for declarer, but East was still singing 'Diamonds are Forever' rather than 'Diamonds are a Girl's Best Friend' and continued the suit to help declarer on her way. South ruffed, played a second heart to the king and led a third round, ruffed in hand. Only now did she lead a third round of clubs. West put in the ten of trumps, forcing dummy's king. Now the last heart was ruffed with the queen of spades, leaving this position:

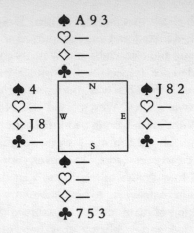

The seven of clubs left the defenders without resource. If West discarded, North would ruff with the three of spades and East would have to overruff and lead away from his tenace. So West bravely threw the four of spades into the fray. The nine was played from dummy and now East had to overruff with the jack and lead from ♠8-2 round to ♠A-3. It is rare that the fate of a contract revolves around the relative positions of the three lowest trump cards!

In this next example, the female declarer demonstrated her flexibility on a hand where the defenders could choose which squeeze they would be subjected to.

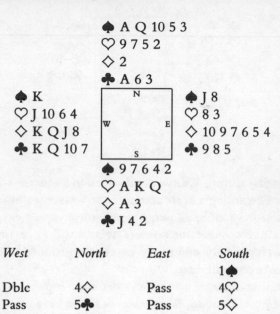

	♠ A Q 10 5 3	
	♡ 9 7 5 2	
	◇ 2	
	♣ A 6 3	
♠ K		♠ J 8
♡ J 10 6 4		♡ 8 3
◇ K Q J 8		◇ 10 9 7 6 5 4
♣ K Q 10 7		♣ 9 8 5
	♠ 9 7 6 4 2	
	♡ A K Q	
	◇ A 3	
	♣ J 4 2	

West	North	East	South
			1♠
Dblc	4◇	Pass	4♡
Pass	5♣	Pass	5◇
Pass	6♠	All Pass	

In a teams-of-four match, South dealt at Love All and opened one spade. West doubled and North bid four diamonds to show a singleton or void in the suit and a raise to four spades. East passed and, after some cue-bidding, North–South could not resist bidding up to six spades.

The king of diamonds was led and South won. Trumps were drawn in two rounds and the diamond ruff was taken. Now the female declarer was careful to cash only two rounds of hearts before running the trumps and arriving at this position:

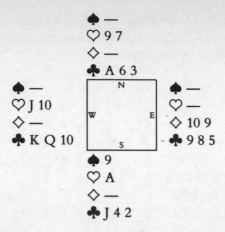

On the last trump, West was subjected to a squeeze without the count. Discarding a heart amounted to immediate surrender, so he discarded a club, allowing South to set up an extra trick in that suit. Note that the squeeze would still have worked had South played only one round or even no rounds of hearts but fails if she plays all three.

But now consider a change in defence. Suppose that, instead of leading a diamond, West starts with the king of clubs. South simply allows it to hold the trick and has thereby rectified the count for a simple squeeze against West. West has to switch at trick two to avoid giving a free finesse and the position reduces to:

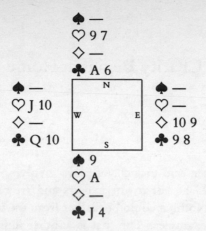

♠ —
♡ 9 7
♢ —
♣ A 6

♠ —   N   ♠ —
♡ J 10   ♡ —
♢ —   W   E   ♢ 10 9
♣ Q 10   S   ♣ 9 8

♠ 9
♡ A
♢ —
♣ J 4

This time, South has the option to cash the ace of hearts first or simply lead the trump immediately. Either way, West has no answer.

14

Charity Begins at Home

It has often been said that clever plays involving endplays and squeezes should be left to the experts and are not part of the female game. Nothing could be further from the truth and there are plenty of examples. The first is another illustration of the advantage of being generous.

In an international women's teams-of-four match, West dealt at Game All.

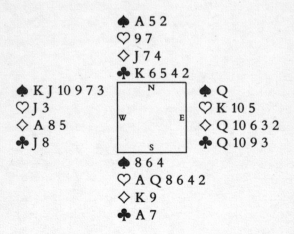

```
                    ♠ A 5 2
                    ♡ 9 7
                    ◇ J 7 4
                    ♣ K 6 5 4 2
  ♠ K J 10 9 7 3        N         ♠ Q
  ♡ J 3                           ♡ K 10 5
  ◇ A 8 5       W         E       ◇ Q 10 6 3 2
  ♣ J 8                           ♣ Q 10 9 3
                       S
                    ♠ 8 6 4
                    ♡ A Q 8 6 4 2
                    ◇ K 9
                    ♣ A 7
```

Room 1

	West	North	East	South
	2◇	Pass	2♠	All Pass

Room 2

	West	North	East	South
	2◇	Pass	2♡	Pass
	2♠	Pass	Pass	3♡
	All Pass			

In both rooms, West opened with a multicoloured two diamonds, almost invariably showing a weak two in either major. North passed and now the bidding diverged. In one room, East bid two spades, expressing the wish to play there if partner had spades but a willingness to play in three hearts if partner had that suit.

Frightened off by the announcement of some heart support in the East hand, South did not enter the bidding and East was allowed to play two spades. Declarer lost one trick in spades, two in hearts, one in diamonds and two in clubs to finish one off.

In the other room, East bid a more conservative two hearts and was corrected to two spades by West. This was passed round to South, who now considered it safe to come in with three hearts, which became the final contract. Declarer could see that it was probable that there were six defensive tricks to be taken against two spades, so it was particularly important for her to justify her bidding.

West led the jack of clubs to South's ace. South cashed her ace of trumps and crossed to the king of clubs to lead another trump. East played the ten and South won with the queen, continuing the suit to drive out the king. East switched to the queen of spades, West overtaking and North's ace winning, the bidding having indicated the 6-1 split. Now came the double loser-on-loser play. The five of clubs was led from dummy and South discarded a spade. East played her last winning club and

South discarded a spade again. Left with nothing but diamonds, East had to open them up and South guessed right (East would surely have bid two spades with eleven points and ♡K-10-x) to land the contract.

The defence, of course, had slipped. Had East risen with the king of hearts and switched to the queen of spades, he could not have been endplayed. North wins with the ace of spades and plays a club but now, if South discards, East can exit with the ten of hearts (before or after playing her other club) and South, stuck in her hand, can take only eight tricks to lose 5 IMPS. In fairness, however, switch the positions of the queen and jack of hearts and those of the ace and king of diamonds, and now rising with the king of hearts would have given away the contract and there was really no way of knowing. Indeed, South's lack of interest in a trump finesse suggested, if anything, that she did not have the queen – female deception strikes yet again!

As the number of cards which have an integral role to play in a hand increases the more interesting the play becomes, as this next hand illustrates. In an international teams–of–four match, South dealt, with North–South vulnerable.

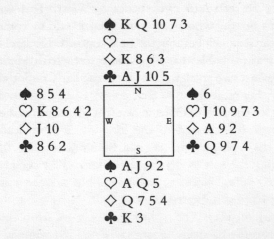

West	North	East	South
			1NT
Pass	2♣	Pass	2♠
Pass	6♠	All Pass	

The dealer opened one no-trump (15–17). With East-West silent, North tried a Stayman inquiry and, on hearing the spade suit, raised to six spades. This was something of a hit-or-miss auction, but nevertheless the two women concerned had landed in a reasonable contract – female intuition again?

West led the jack of diamonds to the three, two and queen. After drawing trumps in three rounds, South combined the chances of finesse and drop in clubs by cashing the ace and king and then running the jack. It was clear to East that declarer was trying to drop the queen so she played the nine smoothly but to no avail, as South discarded a diamond. Now came the *coup de grâce* – a low diamond from dummy, putting East in an impossible position. If she won with the ace, South could claim the rest. If she played low, West would have to win and allow two diamond discards in dummy on the enforced heart return into South's tenace.

Thus there were interesting positions in all three side-suits and it is noteworthy that South played well to refrain from trying a fourth round of clubs, which would have given West the opportunity to disembarrass herself of the blocking ten of diamonds, allowing East to score two tricks in the suit. Covering the jack of clubs would not have helped either. South ruffs and plays a low diamond from both hands; there is no hurry for the discard on the ten of clubs.

In an earlier chapter, a hand was shown in which a king was badly placed, over the queen-jack and under the ace, and was therefore deprived of a trick. That does not mean, however, that kings sitting over aces and under queen-jacks are going to do any better – not with women around anyway! In this next hand, a king seemed destined to take the all-important setting trick but the player holding him was forced to give it up.

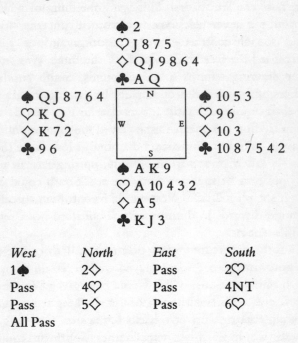

♠ 2
♡ J 8 7 5
♢ Q J 9 8 6 4
♣ A Q

♠ Q J 8 7 6 4
♡ K Q
♢ K 7 2
♣ 9 6

♠ 10 5 3
♡ 9 6
♢ 10 3
♣ 10 8 7 5 4 2

♠ A K 9
♡ A 10 4 3 2
♢ A 5
♣ K J 3

West	North	East	South
1♠	2♢	Pass	2♡
Pass	4♡	Pass	4NT
Pass	5♢	Pass	6♡
All Pass			

In a multiple teams-of-four event, West dealt with East-West vulnerable. The dealer opened one spade. North overcalled with two diamonds and East made a disciplined pass! South bid two hearts, forcing by their methods, and North raised to game. South tried a Blackwood inquiry and on hearing about the ace, confidently bid six hearts, a contract which was reached at very few tables.

Twenty-nine points were on view and, with West having opened the bidding, it was a simple matter for South to place her with all the outstanding honours. West's opening lead was the queen of spades and, when dummy went down, West was delighted to see that the king of diamonds was well placed to beat the contract. It seemed to be a matter of waiting for the big moment. Declarer won the first trick with the ace of spades and laid down the ace of hearts, drawing the king from West. The principle of restricted choice clearly did not apply here and South continued with the king of spades and a spade ruffed *low*. Three rounds of clubs followed and although West refused to ruff, that merely delayed the agony. She was now thrown in with the queen of hearts and had to lead away from the king of diamonds or concede a ruff and discard.

Notice, however, that if South ruffs the third round of spades with the jack of trumps, she may be defeated. Now West does ruff the jack of clubs and exits with a spade. Her partner, with that fabulous zero-count, now makes her sensational entry, being able to overruff dummy and prevent the ruff and discard, leaving South with a diamond to lose after all. However, if declarer does choose this line, she is, on the actual lie of the cards, still safe if she cashes only two rounds of clubs before exiting in trumps.

A ruff and discard allows a declarer to discard a loser on a winning trump, but women are not averse to enjoying success at the other extreme. Watch a declarer humiliate her opponents by discarding a winner on a loser. In a pairs event, West dealt, vulnerable against non-vulnerable opponents.

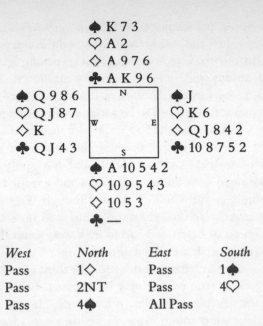

```
                    ♠ K 7 3
                    ♡ A 2
                    ◇ A 9 7 6
                    ♣ A K 9 6
        ♠ Q 9 8 6        N          ♠ J
        ♡ Q J 8 7                   ♡ K 6
        ◇ K        W          E     ◇ Q J 8 4 2
        ♣ Q J 4 3        S          ♣ 10 8 7 5 2
                    ♠ A 10 5 4 2
                    ♡ 10 9 5 4 3
                    ◇ 10 5 3
                    ♣ —
```

West	North	East	South
Pass	1◇	Pass	1♠
Pass	2NT	Pass	4♡
Pass	4♠	All Pass	

He passed and North opened one diamond. East–West were silent and South responded one spade. North rebid two no-trumps and the woman sitting South decided that the hand was now worth game and bid four hearts, which her partner corrected to four spades. She had taken a very rosy view of her four points but two five-card majors were not to be sniffed at and the void was not in her partner's bid suit. She now proceeded to back her judgement with some sparkling play.

West led the queen of clubs, won in dummy, South discarding a diamond. Declarer immediately set about the hearts, playing ace and another. East took the king and returned a club, won in dummy, while South discarded another diamond. Now the king of trumps drew the jack from East, giving an indication that the trumps were breaking badly. South ruffed a club in hand and a heart in dummy, on which East discarded, confirming the trump position beyond all doubt. South now cashed the ace of diamonds and received a further hint of the distribution when

West produced the king. Another club ruff was followed by another heart ruff and, when West followed throughout, he was known to have started with a 4–4–1–4 distribution. All South needed to do now was to play the six of diamonds from dummy and discard a winning heart. West, reduced to three trumps, was forced to ruff and lead away from his tenace to give South eleven tricks and a complete top.

Declarer can, indeed, often save losers in the trump suit by reducing a defender to three trumps. Our next example involves two lowly sevens.

In a women's world championship, North dealt with East–West vulnerable.

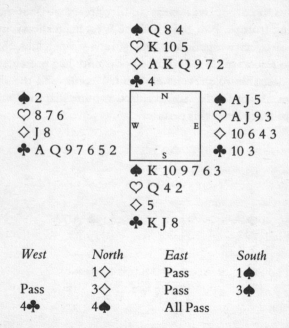

```
              ♠ Q 8 4
              ♡ K 10 5
              ◇ A K Q 9 7 2
              ♣ 4
   ♠ 2                        ♠ A J 5
   ♡ 8 7 6         N          ♡ A J 9 3
   ◇ J 8        W    E        ◇ 10 6 4 3
   ♣ A Q 9 7 6 5 2   S        ♣ 10 3
              ♠ K 10 9 7 6 3
              ♡ Q 4 2
              ◇ 5
              ♣ K J 8
```

West	North	East	South
	1◇	Pass	1♠
Pass	3◇	Pass	3♠
4♣	4♠	All Pass	

The dealer opened one diamond. East passed and South responded with one spade. West now strangely passed and North jumped to three diamonds. East passed and South repeated her spades. Now West came in with four clubs and one wonders why this was delayed a round. It seemed particularly unwise to come in now when the opponents could well have had a bad misfit. As it turned out, North was able to raise to four spades, which became the final contract.

Playing MUD (middle-up-down) leads, West led the seven of hearts to the ten, jack and queen. South continued with dummy's three top diamonds, on which she threw her two remaining hearts as West ruffed the third. West persisted with the eight of hearts, which South ruffed and, to be sure of preventing East from pushing another diamond through, she led the king of clubs to lose the trick to West. West led her last heart and South ruffed; she then led a club, ruffing in dummy.

At this point, it was clear to declarer that East had the remaining trumps. Not only had the West hand shown up with three hearts, two diamonds and surely seven clubs, but the failure to lead a trump when the opportunity had presented itself (surely desirable to prevent club ruffs) confirmed the original singleton. Accordingly, South ruffed another diamond with the ten of spades to leave this position:

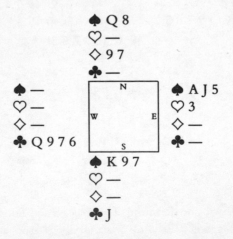

Now South ruffed her last club with dummy's queen of trumps. East overruffed and returned the last heart but now South was able to play the seven of spades, thoughtfully retained for this purpose, and overruff with the eight. At trick twelve, the seven of diamonds was led and East's remaining trumps were caught. Note that, if East refuses to overruff the queen of trumps, South simply plays the eight of spades from dummy, intending to underplay the seven, should East play low.

15

Feeling the Pinch

Turning from the sphere of endplays to that of squeezes: a squeeze is usually thought of as a winning play, made in order to land a difficult contract. However, a squeeze can also operate to gain a crucial overtrick or to avoid an unnecessary undertrick, which is especially useful at matchpointed pairs. On this example, it took a down-to-earth woman to appreciate that a squeeze was needed to restrict her losses and earn herself a substantial number of matchpoints.

In a pairs contest, South dealt at Game All.

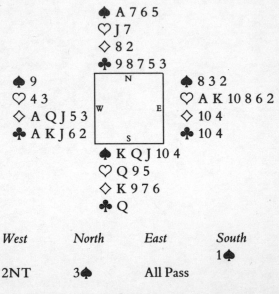

	♠ A 7 6 5	
	♡ J 7	
	◇ 8 2	
	♣ 9 8 7 5 3	

♠ 9		♠ 8 3 2
♡ 4 3		♡ A K 10 8 6 2
◇ A Q J 5 3		◇ 10 4
♣ A K J 6 2		♣ 10 4

	♠ K Q J 10 4	
	♡ Q 9 5	
	◇ K 9 7 6	
	♣ Q	

West	North	East	South
			1♠
2NT	3♠	All Pass	

The dealer opened one spade and West came in with an unusual two no-trumps, promising at least 5–5 in the minors. North competed with three spades and East, with no interest in either minor, felt that she could not bid. The bid was passed back to West, who reluctantly passed. An interesting point arises here: if West does decide to bid, her best shot is probably a take-out double. Having already indicated the two five-card minors, she can now add her 'tolerance' for hearts, if such a holding qualifies for that description! As the cards lie, four hearts by East can be made but not many were likely to bid it and any part-score by East–West would score between 110 and 200.

It was thus clear that South had to try and get out for one rather than two off. West cashed the ace of clubs and, on seeing her partner's distributional ten and declarer's queen, switched to the four of hearts to her partner's king. East now did well to cash the ten of diamonds but then erred by playing another diamond before cashing her ace of hearts (this would have allowed a third – low – diamond from West without enabling dummy to discard a heart loser).

As it was, West played the second heart to her partner's ace and East switched back to clubs. (Sadly, this was another error, as a third heart would have enabled her partner to ruff with the nine of spades, forcing dummy's ace and destroying the entries for the squeeze later.) South ruffed the club and cashed the king and queen of trumps to leave these cards outstanding, five tricks already having been lost:

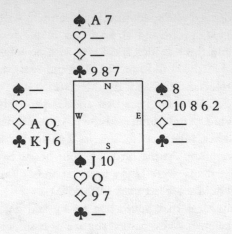

```
              ♠ A 7
              ♡ —
              ◇ —
              ♣ 9 8 7
  ♠ —          ┌──N──┐          ♠ 8
  ♡ —          │     │          ♡ 10 8 6 2
  ◇ A Q      W │     │ E        ◇ —
  ♣ K J 6      │     │          ♣ —
              └──S──┘
              ♠ J 10
              ♡ Q
              ◇ 9 7
              ♣ —
```

Now came the queen of hearts, on which West and North discarded clubs while East followed. On the jack of trumps, West was in trouble. Had she discarded a diamond, the jack would have been allowed to hold, after which South would have ruffed a diamond to set up the nine and claim the rest. So she released the jack of clubs, allowing South to overtake and ruff dummy's clubs high. It is surely a fair bet that this is the first time any player of either sex has successfully brought off an 'overtaking', 'entry-shifting' or 'see-saw' squeeze to go one off in a contract! Admittedly, opponents' bidding and defence left much to be desired, but that does not detract from some scintillating declarer play . . . which was needed after her partner's aggressive bidding!

Turning to variations on the theme, it is also usually thought that the way declarer exerts the pressure of a squeeze on a defender is by cashing a winner. In the next example, a woman shows how to execute a squeeze by playing a loser.

At teams-of-four, South dealt at Game All.

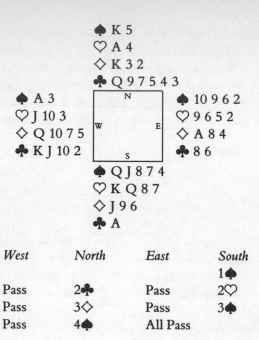

♠ K 5
♡ A 4
◇ K 3 2
♣ Q 9 7 5 4 3

♠ A 3   ♠ 10 9 6 2
♡ J 10 3   ♡ 9 6 5 2
◇ Q 10 7 5   ◇ A 8 4
♣ K J 10 2   ♣ 8 6

♠ Q J 8 7 4
♡ K Q 8 7
◇ J 9 6
♣ A

West	North	East	South
			1♠
Pass	2♣	Pass	2♡
Pass	3◇	Pass	3♠
Pass	4♠	All Pass	

The dealer opened one spade. East–West were silent throughout
and North responded two clubs. When South rebid two hearts,
North decided that K-x-x was not enough in diamonds to bid
no-trumps out of hand and in any case, if partner held ◇Q-x,
she would want the declaration to come from the other side.
Accordingly, she bid a fourth suit forcing three diamonds. This
gave South a problem. Most players would probably have
looked at the general nature of their hand and bid three no-
trumps – a contract which stands little chance on the actual
layout – but our declarer was worried about not holding a full
diamond stopper and chose to rebid three spades instead, which
North raised to game.

The bidding strongly invited a diamond lead, and West duly
obliged. Sadly, this was the only lead which gave declarer a
chance. Dummy played low and East won, after which she
switched to a trump. This cost a trick in that suit but prevented

two potential red-suit ruffs in dummy, after which South would lose two tricks but no more. West took the ace of trumps and returned the suit, dummy's king winning. South returned to hand with the ace of clubs, drew the remaining two trumps, crossed to the ace of hearts and ruffed a club with her last trump. Now the king and queen of hearts were cashed to leave this position:

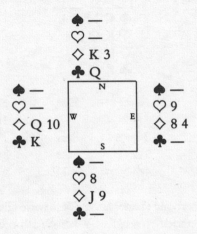

On the eight of hearts, West was finished. Whichever suit she discarded, dummy would discard the other and East, on winning the heart, would have to return a diamond to dummy's king and the established winner.

Of course, not only are women capable throughout the squeeze spectrum; they have just as much fun spoiling them for others. On this next hand, a female defender cut the communication cord.

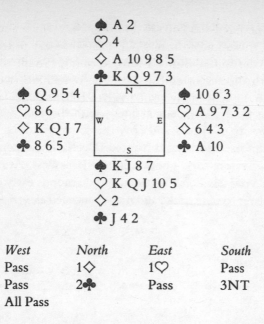

                    ♠ A 2
                    ♡ 4
                    ◇ A 10 9 8 5
                    ♣ K Q 9 7 3

♠ Q 9 5 4   N   ♠ 10 6 3
♡ 8 6   ♡ A 9 7 3 2
◇ K Q J 7   W   E   ◇ 6 4 3
♣ 8 6 5   ♣ A 10
                    S

                    ♠ K J 8 7
                    ♡ K Q J 10 5
                    ◇ 2
                    ♣ J 4 2

West	North	East	South
Pass	1◇	1♡	Pass
Pass	2♣	Pass	3NT
All Pass			

In a major pairs contest, West dealt at Love All. At most tables, the final contract was three no-trumps by South, reached after East had overcalled North's one-diamond opening with one heart. At pairs, players tend to overcall, especially when non-vulnerable, on these very weak hands and it sometimes pays but, particularly on such very poor suits, one has to be prepared that these bids will often give more help to the opponents.

At one table, West dutifully led the eight of hearts and East ducked it to South's queen. South continued the suit with the king and this time East won and made the error of continuing with the seven, West discarding a low club to indicate a diamond holding in the McKenney style. South won with the ten and played a club to the king and East's ace. Clearly unable to continue hearts, East now switched to a diamond to West's jack and North's ace. On the run of the clubs, both defenders were obliged to come down to two spades to avoid conceding a red-suit trick. Thus South took three spade tricks and a heart at the end to score 460 for an excellent board.

At the woman's table, West again led the eight of hearts. East also ducked this to South's queen and refused again when South continued with the king of hearts. South now switched to clubs. East won and, anticipating trouble later on, switched to the three of spades. When she came in with the ace of hearts, she played the six of spades and now the communication necessary for the squeeze had been disrupted. Declarer was consequently held to ten tricks for a good score to East–West. After North's opening, very few defenders attacked diamonds early enough to hold declarer to nine tricks and most conceded eleven.

Cornering

Women's skills in both the endplay and squeeze areas have been demonstrated, so the time has come to combine the two. In this first example, the declarer took advantage of an ill-judged duck at trick one.

The late Maurice Harrison-Gray was always very keen on cashing a long suit early in a no-trump contract to force the defenders into early decisions on their discarding. This is not an idea exclusively held by men.

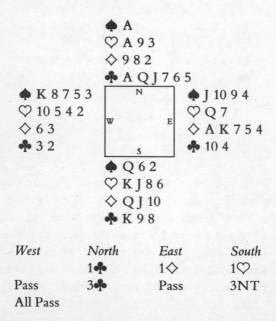

West	North	East	South
	1♣	1◇	1♡
Pass	3♣	Pass	3NT
All Pass			

In a pairs contest, North dealt at Love All and opened a natural one club. East overcalled with one diamond and South bid one heart. East passed and, when North jumped to three clubs, South bid three no-trumps, the final contract.

West dutifully led the six of diamonds and East, trying to keep communications open, thought that ducking was in order. In the context of the diamond suit, alone, this was perfectly correct but, looking at the whole hand, she might have thought twice. It was clear that a string of clubs was coming, on which both she and her partner would have to find at least four discards each. Observe what happened. South won the diamond and reeled off her six club tricks, forcing the defenders to reduce to this position:

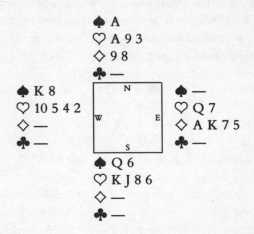

West had been obliged to discard his second diamond to keep his major-suit holdings intact, ruining any hope of enjoying East's diamonds. Now South cashed dummy's ace of spades and played the ace and a second heart to the queen and king, before exiting with the queen of spades to force West to lead round to the heart tenace and give declarer a twelfth trick. Had East taken the first two tricks, there obviously would have been only eleven.

This type of situation occurs more frequently than many people realize. Another example follows in which the female declarer took advantage of a defender who failed to lead through strength.

In an international teams-of-four match, North dealt at Love All.

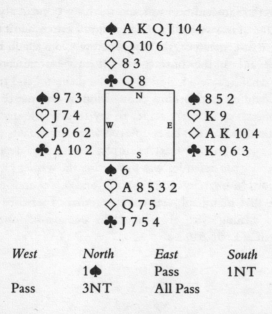

```
                    ♠ A K Q J 10 4
                    ♡ Q 10 6
                    ◇ 8 3
                    ♣ Q 8
    ♠ 9 7 3              N           ♠ 8 5 2
    ♡ J 7 4                          ♡ K 9
    ◇ J 9 6 2      W         E       ◇ A K 10 4
    ♣ A 10 2                         ♣ K 9 6 3
                         S
                    ♠ 6
                    ♡ A 8 5 3 2
                    ◇ Q 7 5
                    ♣ J 7 5 4
```

West	North	East	South
	1♠	Pass	1NT
Pass	3NT	All Pass	

East–West were silent at both tables and in one room North opened one spade. When her partner responded with one no-trump, she quietly bid two spades, making nine tricks when the defenders cashed their minor-suit winners early. At the other table, North was carried away by her solid spades and raised one no-trump to three no-trumps. Well, at least, that had more chance than four of a major!

When West led the two of diamonds, split honours in the suit would have led to an immediate two-trick defeat, but luck was in for South when East cashed her two honours and cleared the suit. Now followed the inevitable six rounds of spades and, with declarer placing East with the king of hearts and West with the jack, there was no defence. Both defenders had to keep two hearts and two minor-suit winners and at trick ten South exited with the eight of clubs. West cashed her two tricks and then had to open up the hearts to dummy's ten and East's misery. In fairness to the pair who stopped in the part-score, the game needed both diamond honours and the king of hearts with East and the jack of hearts with West and even then a spade lead is still likely to defeat the contract. Indeed, so would a spade switch at trick two – at best, the contract was a twenty-to-one shot!

When defending in this kind of situation, it will usually pay to blank honours at an early stage, to try to give the declarer the impression that you can be endplayed whereas, in fact, you have been squeezed. In this next example, the female declarer got home because the defender was protecting the wrong king.

The word 'monarchy' implies 'one' and it is therefore understandable that many subjects have minimal experience when it comes to dealing with two kings! In a teams-of-four match, South dealt at Love All.

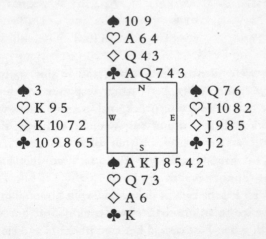

West	North	East	South
			1♠
Pass	2♣	Pass	4♠
Pass	6♠	All Pass	

The dealer opened one spade and, with East–West silent throughout, North responded with two clubs. South jumped to four spades and North raised to six spades.

West tried the deceptive-looking lead of the eight of clubs and South paused to ask herself why West had failed to touch one of the unbid red suits. She also correctly reasoned that West would not have risked helping to set up dummy's long suit unless she herself was also long in clubs. She also noticed that West had avoided a trump lead which suggested that either she had the queen or perhaps a singleton or void.

South won the first trick with the king of clubs and cashed one high trump. She now crossed to the ace of hearts and discarded a small heart on the ace of clubs. The queen of clubs was ruffed by East and overruffed.

A point of interest arises here in respect of East's defence. If he refuses to ruff, South will ask herself why and probably guess the spade position. However, if East has just two low trumps, it will be very good play to refuse to ruff. This allows South another discard but declarer will now almost certainly misguess the spade position and lose a diamond at the end.

As the play went, the spade problem was solved and South reeled off the rest of the trumps. West blanked his king of hearts, keeping the king of diamonds protected, and was thrown in with the heart to lead into the split diamond tenace. With the king of hearts already a master, West might have done better to discard the other way. His black suit count was known but he could possibly have been 1–2–5–5, in which case the contract might have been defeated, depending on South's opinion of West's skill.

17

Battle on the Plain

The hand which follows demonstrates above all others the superiority of women over men. The religious-minded will remember a regular late-night radio programme, *Lighten Our Darkness*.

Can anything give more satisfaction than a player looking at twenty-six cards outperforming 'expert' kibitzers, who can see all fifty-two?

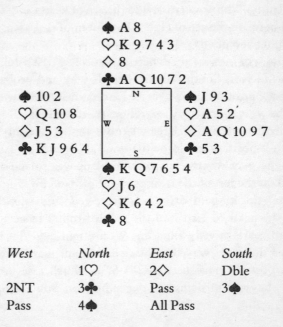

	♠ A 8	
	♡ K 9 7 4 3	
	◇ 8	
	♣ A Q 10 7 2	

♠ 10 2		♠ J 9 3
♡ Q 10 8	N	♡ A 5 2
◇ J 5 3	W E	◇ A Q 10 9 7
♣ K J 9 6 4	S	♣ 5 3

	♠ K Q 7 6 5 4	
	♡ J 6	
	◇ K 6 4 2	
	♣ 8	

West	*North*	*East*	*South*
	1♡	2◇	Dble
2NT	3♣	Pass	3♠
Pass	4♠	All Pass	

In an international teams-of-four match played on Vu–Graph under the scrutiny of male 'expert' commentators, North dealt, vulnerable against non-vulnerable opponents, and opened one heart. East overcalled two diamonds and South made a negative double. This is a little surprising but, with the partnership playing five-card majors, it was presumably an attempt to offer both majors in case her partner had six hearts and very few spades. West competed with two no-trumps, showing a raise to three diamonds with moderate values, and North bid three clubs. East passed and now South introduced her spade suit, which North raised to game.

West led the three of diamonds to her partner's ace and East tried to force the dummy by returning the suit. South ruffed in dummy and now the 'experts' expected her to lead a heart, eventually taking the club finesse to dispose of her last diamond, making the contract for the loss of two hearts and a diamond. The declarer, however, could not see the king of clubs and confined herself to working on the assumption that the ace of hearts was with East. She cashed the ace of clubs and ruffed a club, returning to the ace of trumps to ruff a third club. When East showed out, the distribution in that suit was revealed and with the diamonds known to be 5–3, a complete count on the hand was available as South reeled off her trumps.

By the end of trick eight, East was down to three diamonds and two hearts and the last trump executed the endplay-squeeze. If she threw another diamond, South would play king and another in that suit to force her to lead away from the ace of hearts. She therefore preferred to discard the five of hearts, blanking her ace, after which South played a low heart from both hands to set up the king for her tenth trick. This, as the experts admitted afterwards, was a clearly superior line to the club finesse, although West's bidding and East's early defence both suggested that the king of clubs would be well placed for declarer.

The most interesting hands from the bridge writer's point of view are those where there is scope for good play on both sides. This example occurred in a women's teams-of-four match, East dealt, non-vulnerable against vulnerable opponents.

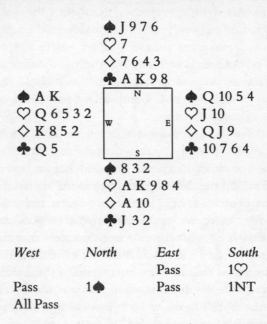

♠ J 9 7 6
♡ 7
♢ 7 6 4 3
♣ A K 9 8

♠ A K
♡ Q 6 5 3 2
♢ K 8 5 2
♣ Q 5

♠ Q 10 5 4
♡ J 10
♢ Q J 9
♣ 10 7 6 4

♠ 8 3 2
♡ A K 9 8 4
♢ A 10
♣ J 3 2

West	North	East	South
		Pass	1♡
Pass	1♠	Pass	1NT
All Pass			

East passed and South opened one heart. West passed and North responded one spade. South rebid one no-trump and all passed.

West led the two of diamonds to the three, jack and ace and declarer set about the spades, losing the first round to West's king. The five of diamonds went to East's queen and the nine was overtaken by West, who cashed the eight. Declarer threw two low hearts and East the jack of hearts. The first good play of the hand now came from West, who, far-sightedly fearing a throw-in, now cashed her ace of spades before switching to a low heart to the ten and ace. These cards remained with the defenders having won five tricks to date:

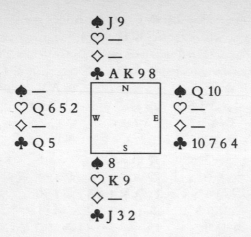

♠ J 9
♥ —
♦ —
♣ A K 9 8

♠ —   ♠ Q 10
♥ Q 6 5 2   ♥ —
♦ —   ♦ —
♣ Q 5   ♣ 10 7 6 4

♠ 8
♥ K 9
♦ —
♣ J 3 2

On the ace of clubs West was threatened again. Playing low would allow a low club to endplay her in hearts and on the second round of that suit, East would be squeezed in the black suits. So West made her second good play by unblocking queen of clubs. Sadly, South had an answer. She played a low club to the jack, cashed the king of hearts and now East was in trouble. A club discard would amount to immediate surrender so she threw the ten of spades. Now a spade to the queen forced her to lead round the North's clubs for seven tricks despite West's efforts – great play all round!

One brilliant defence unrewarded is followed by another which should have suffered similar treatment. At teams–of–four, North dealt at Game All.

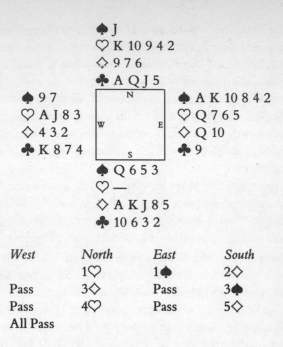

♠ J
♡ K 10 9 4 2
♦ 9 7 6
♣ A Q J 5

♠ 9 7
♡ A J 8 3
♦ 4 3 2
♣ K 8 7 4

N
W E
S

♠ A K 10 8 4 2
♡ Q 7 6 5
♦ Q 10
♣ 9

♠ Q 6 5 3
♡ —
♦ A K J 8 5
♣ 10 6 3 2

West	North	East	South
	1♡	1♠	2♦
Pass	3♦	Pass	3♠
Pass	4♡	Pass	5♦
All Pass			

The dealer opened one heart. East overcalled with one spade and South bid two diamonds, which her partner raised to three diamonds. With her intolerance of hearts, South should probably have left it at that but she attempted to look for three no-trumps with the directional asking bid of three spades. Unable to oblige, North repeated her hearts (surely four clubs would have been more descriptive) and South now had to settle for five diamonds.

West was on lead and, with the other three suits well held, should have led a trump which would probably have beaten the contract outright but she decided to respect her partner's bid and preferred the nine of spades. East won with the king and returned the ten of diamonds to South's ace. A spade was now ruffed in dummy, a heart was ruffed in hand and another spade was led for a further ruff.

What was West to discard? If she threw a heart, play would continue as follows: dummy ruffs the spade, South ruffs another heart, takes a club finesse, ruffs a third heart, dropping West's ace. Now the king of trumps is cashed, a second club finesse taken and high hearts are cashed until West ruffs with the last trump. She now has to lead to the split tenace in clubs. If West discards a club, South draws trumps and runs the ten of clubs to enjoy the whole suit without difficulty, quietly conceding a heart at the end.

To save the day, West 'discarded' a trump. South should still have succeeded by overruffing, returning with a heart ruff and drawing the last trump on which dummy discards a heart. On the next trump, West is strip-squeezed in this position:

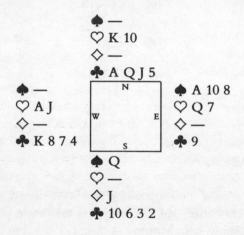

If she discards a heart, so does dummy and then South takes the club finesse and exits in hearts, leaving West to continue clubs. If she discards a club, dummy still discards a heart and South runs the ten of clubs to bring in the whole suit, again conceding a heart at the end.

However, at the table, South actually discarded a club from dummy too early and West could now safely discard a club on the last trump and take her two heart tricks.

Another female declarer demonstrated that underruffing can be countered in this next example. At teams-of-four, South dealt at Game All.

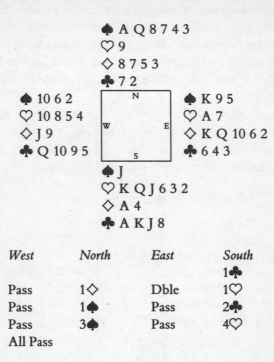

```
                    ♠ A Q 8 7 4 3
                    ♡ 9
                    ◇ 8 7 5 3
                    ♣ 7 2
    ♠ 10 6 2            N            ♠ K 9 5
    ♡ 10 8 5 4                       ♡ A 7
    ◇ J 9        W          E        ◇ K Q 10 6 2
    ♣ Q 10 9 5                       ♣ 6 4 3
                         S
                    ♠ J
                    ♡ K Q J 6 3 2
                    ◇ A 4
                    ♣ A K J 8
```

West	North	East	South
			1♣
Pass	1◇	Dble	1♡
Pass	1♠	Pass	2♣
Pass	3♠	Pass	4♡
All Pass			

The dealer opened a strong one club. West passed and North replied with one diamond, showing less than eight points. East doubled to show her diamond suit and South bid one heart. Thereafter, East–West remained silent and North bid one spade, South two clubs and North three spades. South might then have been advised to go for game in spades to make maximum use of her partner's hand but she preferred four hearts, which became the final contract.

West led the jack of diamonds. South won and advanced the jack of spades. When West ducked smoothly, South used Zia Mahmood's 'Roll over Houdini' tip, 'If (s)he does not cover, (s)he has not got it', and rose with the ace of spades. She now ruffed a spade and cashed two top clubs before ruffing a third round in dummy. After ruffing a further spade, she exited with a diamond, which East won to leave this position:

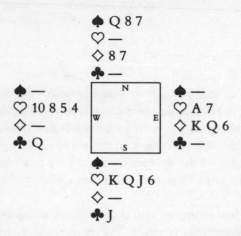

East played another diamond, which South ruffed high. To ensure that her partner could win the next trick, West played very well to underruff. On the jack of clubs, West played the queen and her partner ruffed with the seven of hearts before exiting with yet another diamond. Again South ruffed high and now had to realize that her only realistic hope was that the ace of trumps would now fall. She duly played a low trump to land the contract. Note that if West fails to underruff, she makes the position much clearer – again excellent play on both sides!

18

Rose-coloured Spectacles

Most of the deals that we have seen previously involve reasonable bidding to reasonable contracts. It is not always the case that such accurate bidding prevails, whether it is men or women who are responsible. When dummy is revealed to be less suitable than declarer had hoped for, it is necessary to keep one's head and do the best in the circumstances – in addition, perhaps, to reciting a silent prayer.

The next few examples will show women using all their skill to land some dubious contracts. At teams-of-four, East dealt at Love All.

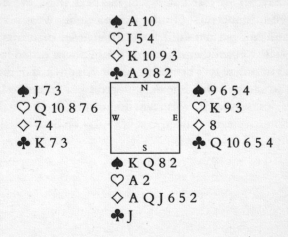

West	North	East	South
		Pass	1◇
Pass	2♣	Pass	2♠
Pass	4◇	Pass	4♡
Pass	5♣	Pass	6♠
Pass	7◇	All Pass	

East–West were silent throughout and South opened one diamond. North bid two clubs and South reversed into two spades. As this was game-forcing, all North needed to do was to give preference to three diamonds, but she wished to show some real enthusiasm both for diamonds and for playing in a slam, so she jumped to four diamonds. South cue-bid four hearts and North five clubs. It appears that South must have thought that North's previous four-diamond call agreed spades, for she jumped to six spades, only realizing that there was a misunderstanding when North corrected to seven diamonds.

West led a heart to South's ace. Declarer drew trumps in two rounds and paused to take stock. It was clear that the spade suit would have to provide four tricks so it seemed sensible to go for the percentage play – a first-round finesse. So, holding her breath, she played a low spade to the ten. This enabled two heart discards in dummy and two heart ruffs to make the contract. Bad card-holders will be quick to point out that it does not pay to be too greedy. One wonders how the play would have gone had the positions of the eight and nine of spades been exchanged!

Women's magazines are full of tips on 'how to find your man'. One of the world's leading women players many years ago picked up a two-count and was propelled into a slam following another bidding misunderstanding. Her 'man' was the king of trumps and she had to resort to smoking him out.

In a teams contest, North dealt at Game All.

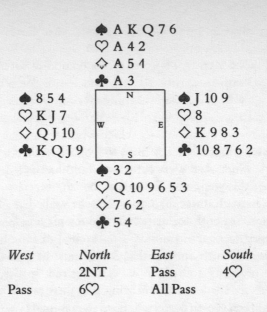

♠ A K Q 7 6
♡ A 4 2
◇ A 5 4
♣ A 3

♠ 8 5 4
♡ K J 7
◇ Q J 10
♣ K Q J 9

N
W   E
S

♠ J 10 9
♡ 8
◇ K 9 8 3
♣ 10 8 7 6 2

♠ 3 2
♡ Q 10 9 6 5 3
◇ 7 6 2
♣ 5 4

West	North	East	South
	2NT	Pass	4♡
Pass	6♡	All Pass	

She opened two no-trumps, showing 20–22 and, with East–West silent, South 'signed off' in four hearts. North, however, took this as a mild slam try and with her wealth of controls, accepted with six hearts.

West led the king of clubs and South realized she needed miracles. She won in dummy and cashed the three top spades, discarding her losing club while the others mercifully followed. It was now a question of how to tackle the trumps. The best line of play in the heart suit, without other considerations, is to play ace and another. This succeeds on any 2–2 or 3–1 break unless West has started with K-J-x (a 4–0 break would have meant defeat in any event). However, on this particular deal there was more to consider. If trumps broke 2–2 there would be no problem, thanks to declarer's lowly three, which could later be played to dummy's four, but if either defender held K-x-x, with or without the jack, they would win the king and play a diamond, removing dummy's only entry prematurely.

In order to improve communications with dummy, declarer

started by playing the two of hearts and, when East played the eight smoothly, South inserted the ten, losing to West's jack. West defended well by switching to a diamond, forcing dummy's ace. South now ruffed a club and led the nine of hearts, West playing the seven, and the moment of truth had arrived.

There were two possibilities for declarer to consider: first, that the trumps were breaking 2–2, which would mean that East had played low without a flicker from K-8 on the previous round of the suit; second, that West held K-J-7 and had failed to notice that he could guarantee defeating the contract by covering South's nine with the king. It is at times like this that a woman's skill in assessing the strength of her opponents is important and our declarer decided to play West for a misdefence. She ran the nine of hearts and, when East showed out, she had made her slam.

With bidding being a language which, to this day, is scarcely out of the cradle, tales of woe in the medium of partnership understanding abound in both sexes and at all levels of the game. Indeed, it is argued that top-class players, who seem to be using an increasing number of two-, three- or multi-purpose bids, are the most prone. One is surely less likely to have a misunderstanding in Dutch than in Double-Dutch!

However, this next hand did not take place in such elevated circles. It occurred at the rubber bridge table, the woman concerned dealing as South at Game All.

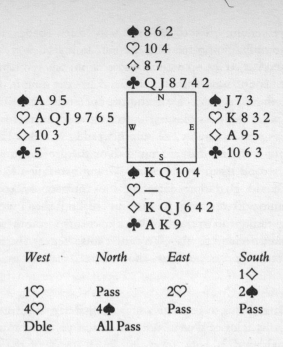

♠ 8 6 2
♡ 10 4
♢ 8 7
♣ Q J 8 7 4 2

♠ A 9 5
♡ A Q J 9 7 6 5
♢ 10 3
♣ 5

♠ J 7 3
♡ K 8 3 2
♢ A 9 5
♣ 10 6 3

♠ K Q 10 4
♡ —
♢ K Q J 6 4 2
♣ A K 9

West	North	East	South
			1♢
1♡	Pass	2♡	2♠
4♡	4♠	Pass	Pass
Dble	All Pass		

South's hand was strong enough to open two diamonds, showing eight playing tricks in that suit, but in rubber bridge circles, the negative response to that bid is two no-trumps, which would have made it difficult for South to continue the description of her hand. She therefore contented herself with opening one diamond. Opinions differ as to the best action on West's hand, but he obviously belonged to the school which believes that a hand containing two aces is too strong to pre-empt and he also 'proceeded quietly' with one heart. North passed and East raised to two hearts, swinging the spotlight back on to South.

In most regular partnerships, the best action would surely be a take-out double. However, at the rubber bridge table where partner is often an unknown quantity, such actions carry a certain amount of risk and South preferred to bid two spades. As it turned out, the two-spade bid carried a risk all of its own, as

North played his partner to hold a five-card spade suit and, when West bid four hearts, he went on to four spades.

West expressed his opinion of this auction, before he had seen either of his opponents' hands, with a confident double. Had he led a heart, his confidence would have been rewarded. The best that declarer can do if she is trying to make her contract is to ruff the opening lead and play the king of spades. If West makes the mistake of winning this, he has to be careful because declarer will discard on the next heart and West must now switch to a minor suit to lock declarer in her hand – a further round of hearts would allow declarer to succeed by ruffing in dummy and finessing the ten of spades. If West ducks the king of spades, what is declarer to do? If she plays on clubs, West ruffs the third round of the suit, cashes the ace of spades and plays hearts and all declarer will make is the queen of spades – five down; if she plays on diamonds she will make one more trick.

If declarer plays to go as few down as possible right from the start, she will discard on both the first two hearts. If West persists with a third heart, declarer can escape for one down by playing a spade to the ten and continuing spades. However, if West plays a club at this stage, he will score a club ruff as well as two hearts and two aces and declarer must go two down.

Fortunately for declarer, West's defensive campaign did not involve any thoughts of trying to force declarer. He preferred to try for a club ruff himself. He therefore led his singleton, intending to win the ace of trumps and put his partner in with his presumed king of hearts.

Declarer now had a chance to shine. Winning the club lead in hand, she played the queen of spades immediately and West erroneously decided to duck. South now switched to the king of diamonds, which was won by East, who now gave his partner the club ruff. The ace of hearts now came much too late. On ruffing, South cashed two more diamonds, discarding a heart from dummy so that any further force in that suit could be taken there. West refused to ruff with his now bare ace of trumps and

South realized that the suit had been divided 3–3.

Accordingly, she exited with the ten of trumps, forcing West to win and return a heart. South ruffed in dummy and attacked clubs. East could ruff whenever he wished, but South overruffed and her diamonds won the rest of the tricks. The poor defence was punished by a superb display of trump control.

The last laugh, of course, belonged to North, enjoying his four-spade bid as he added 790 to the score!

It has been emphasized many times that, when a declarer is in a hopeless contract, he or she should play for the cards to lie favourably. The declarer in this next example played well to give herself the chance of two bites at the cherry.

In a world teams–of–four preliminary round, East dealt at Love All.

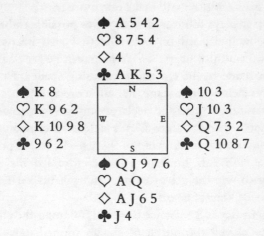

♠ A 5 4 2
♡ 8 7 5 4
♦ 4
♣ A K 5 3

♠ K 8   ♠ 10 3
♡ K 9 6 2   ♡ J 10 3
♦ K 10 9 8   ♦ Q 7 3 2
♣ 9 6 2   ♣ Q 10 8 7

♠ Q J 9 7 6
♡ A Q
♦ A J 6 5
♣ J 4

West	North	East	South
		Pass	1♠
Pass	3NT	Pass	4♣
Pass	4♡	Pass	4NT
Pass	5♡	Pass	6♠
All Pass			

With East–West silent throughout, South opened one spade and North responded with three no-trumps. This was a game-forcing bid, showing a raise to four spades with a singleton and possible slam ambitions. South bid four clubs, an inquiry and North's four hearts showed the diamond singleton, the idea being to avoid bidding the actual suit in order to avoid a double and possible sacrifice. South now tried Blackwood and, on hearing two aces, plunged into the slam, missed at three other tables.

West led the ten of diamonds (unlikely to cost with a singleton announced on the table) and South took East's queen with the ace. Realizing that there was a lot of work to be done, South appreciated that the trumps would have to be breaking 2–2 and that at least one major-suit finesse would have to work. She led the jack of spades and West covered (surely unwise as East might have had a singleton queen). Still playing on the assumption of a 2–2 trump split, South now called for a low club from the table. East took her queen and returned a heart. South was now able to spurn the heart finesse (which was worse than a 50 per cent chance because, some of the time, East would have doubled when she held the king of hearts) and discard her two red-suit losers on the ace and king of clubs. Had the queen of clubs turned out to be with West, the heart finesse would still have been available.

One of the principal sources of argument between men and women is in the question of priorities. Men will surely feel thoroughly humiliated at this female demonstration of the unimportance of trump control.

In a pairs event, South dealt at Love All.

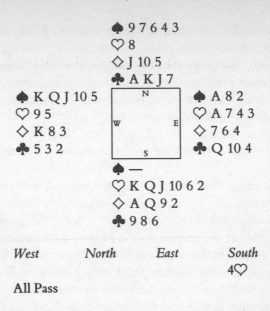

♠ 9 7 6 4 3
♡ 8
◇ J 10 5
♣ A K J 7

♠ K Q J 10 5
♡ 9 5
◇ K 8 3
♣ 5 3 2

♠ A 8 2
♡ A 7 4 3
◇ 7 6 4
♣ Q 10 4

♠ —
♡ K Q J 10 6 2
◇ A Q 9 2
♣ 9 8 6

West	North	East	South
			4♡

All Pass

The woman sitting South was not in the mood for a long conversation, so she opened with four hearts, which she was allowed to play against male opposition.

West made the obvious lead of the king of spades. South ruffed, crossed to the ace of clubs and ran the jack of diamonds, losing to West's king. West persisted with spades and South ruffed again. She now attacked trumps, East winning the first round and producing a third round of spades to reduce South to two trumps while he still had three. But never mind! The woman's ability to improvise came into its own, such petty contingencies as losing trump control were taken in her stride as she carried on regardless! South simply drew two more rounds of trumps, leaving the seven at large in East's hand, and started to cash winning diamonds. East was now caught between the devil and deep blue sea. If he ruffed the last round of diamonds, he would have to lead into dummy's club tenace. If he didn't, he would have to discard a club and dummy's king of clubs would score the tenth trick while he would have simply exchanged his queen of clubs for a trump trick.

Of course, South could have adopted the less spectacular line of discarding a club on the second round of spades so that East would run out after the third round, but it was much more fun to give him the reins, wasn't it?

Conclusion

In the preceding pages, we have seen countless examples of women playing with consummate skill in every area of the game. They clearly have the ability to play just as well as the men. In order to win at bridge, it is not sufficient to be able to play one hand well; it is more important to be able to string together a series of good scores. This is a question of confidence. Bridge is a very complex game and any player, whether male or female, learns only gradually to appreciate the finer points. Most people remember the first time they played a squeeze and how good it made them feel to execute such a play. This gives them the confidence to make the same play over and over again. Success leads to success, and then more success. Women are only just beginning to gain the confidence needed to win consistently. The more women see themselves, and other women, achieving good results at all levels of competition, the more confident they will feel. Although women are not yet winning many of the top-level international encounters, they are making steady progress in that direction and I am sure will continue to do so.

What of the future? As in many other spheres of activity, women are coming from behind but are rapidly narrowing the gap. In the World Junior (under twenty-five years old) Championship held in the USA in the summer of 1991, the winning American team contained two women – a clear indication that the future is bright for the continued improvement and success of women bridge players.